REFURBISHED

THE CLOVER INITIATIVE

MICHELLE MONÁRREZ

Printed in the United States of America.

First Printing, 2020.

Published by Michelle Monárrez

Print ISBN: 978-1-7354899-0-2

E-book ISBN: 978-1-7354899-1-9

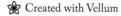 Created with Vellum

To Manuel, my star knight and the love of my life.

"That person who helps others simply because it's the right thing to do, is without a doubt, a real superhero."
-Stan Lee

CRIMSON_

Her father kept skeletons in his closet. The skull of one, to be precise. Alyssa suspected the skull was made from different bodies. The cap of a braincase here, a jaw there, an eye socket over there. Sometimes, she'd close her eyes and call the image of those bones forward. The memory came back the same every time. Burned, curated bones. A chipped smile on a skewed jaw. Empty eye sockets staring back at her. A choked scream in her throat. The bone pieces always fit like a macabre puzzle.

The reason her father kept the skull eluded her. Maybe it was a memento of his days in medical school before his prolific career in the new field of Genetics and Defense Research. Perhaps he needed it to never forget the darker days.

The few times he spoke of The War, he'd said there was a shortage of everything, but a surplus of death. After the ships fell from the sky, her father's career launched through the exploration of the technology left behind. He built the rest of it dreaming up ways to protect the Earth, but almost twenty years passed with the atmosphere staying clear of threats. The skull stayed in the back of a closet, collecting dust, Alyssa still unaware of its purpose.

When she thought of the records hidden in her desk, Alyssa knew she was following his example. She, too, kept skeletons. Files and pictures of them, to be precise. She kept reports of cases she'd worked as an intern in the UK. They represented an opportunity for a brilliant career once, and the life she could have had.

The light of her floating monitor strained her eyes. She finished reading a case report from her new job with the Delta Unit. Alyssa closed her eyes and massaged them with her fingertips. When was the last time she'd had a break? She scanned the gray office. The rows of desks behind hers were empty, and all other floating monitors were off. The screen wall on the back of the Records Room displayed the time with digital green numbers: 11:03 pm. No wonder she was alone. She'd lost track of time trying to catch up on her assignment.

I should call it a night, Alyssa thought. The old case files she had to read would still be there the next day. She should go home, have a shower, a cup of tea, and curl into bed. She needed to be well-rested and alert for another day of getting acquainted with her new Unit's line of work.

Alyssa's gaze shifted to her desk's cabinets. She could go home, or she could have a look at what hid inside her desk.

With another glance around the empty room, Alyssa decided. "Just a quick look."

After setting aside the Unit's papers and records approved for shredding, Alyssa pulled out her old case files. Five manilla folders hid under printer paper, an over-sized stapler, and other meaningless office supplies. Alyssa picked the report on the last case she interned for before transferring to the US. Opening the folder, she jumped back into pictures and records of a crime scene.

More than she wanted to admit, this was developing into a routine. Every time she was alone in the Records Room, she'd whip out her old case records. These and other official documentation could not leave the Records Room, but she could keep them at her desk. There were no exact rules against reading cases her current Unit had never been assigned to. The rules weren't clear about trying to solve them, either.

The Camden Trials scene. A rave in the North of London that went wrong in the most fatal sense of the word. Law enforcement walked into mummified corpses. The first call they made was to Clover Co.'s private Military Department; Enhanced cases were their jurisdiction. Alyssa's old Unit arrived at the scene as the support and cleanup crew. At the time, she was still part of Clover's Military Academy and on track to graduate under the Enhanced Narcotics Division. She took those pictures herself.

As she read through the report, Alyssa brushed off the goosebumps on her arms but couldn't ignore the chill in her bones. The door of the Records Room opened with a soft hiss, and Alyssa's heart jumped to her throat.

"I had a feeling I'd find you here, Crimson." Through the door squeezed James Kings, the leader of her new Unit.

Alyssa quit her frantic efforts to hide her case files. When she first met James three months ago, she would have hidden them from him, but not anymore.

"Don't barge in here like that! You scared me." Heat rose to her cheeks, tinting them with a bronze glow. She placed a hand over her chest, trying to calm her racing heart. "And don't call me that. I'm off the clock." Getting called by her code name wasn't uncommon, but code names were for military functions and field missions. She'd rather be herself closer to midnight.

"And yet you're still here. You should be home."

Alyssa snorted back a laugh. James liked to give her a hard

time about working long hours, even though he did the same. "Look who's talking."

James towered closer to her desk, a relaxed smirk resting on his face. "You should take advantage of shorter shifts while you still can, rookie." His golden gaze darted from her to the files she'd been looking at. The corner of his mouth twitched in revulsion. "Still looking over those Enhanced Narcotics cases?"

"Just reminiscing over some old pictures and my own scribblings."

"Hm... May I?"

Alyssa pushed the documents in front of him. He'd seen them many times before in the last three months. It didn't seem to matter to James, though. Every time he picked them up, he took the time to read them, and Alyssa appreciated him for it.

"This is new." James read on. "You think these five cases had something to do with the same drug." He put the papers down. "Bright Stones?"

"Yeah." Alyssa shrugged. "I have a theory."

"Well, what are you waiting for? Run it by me."

"Okay." Her pulse picked up as she took the folder back. "The postmortem effects were what connected all victims to the same drug. I also thought the environment was favorable for the consumption of it."

Alyssa recalled the locations where the parties took place. Celebrity mansions, high-end exclusive clubs, and underground venues featured parties that ended in a similar fashion to the Camden Trials scene. Ravers overdosed in a matter of minutes; the victim figures rose by dozens. All had collapsed lungs, all disfigured, all with leathery parchment for skin.

James scratched his chin. "But many Enhanced drugs have the same effects, and the venues are far too different in style to connect to a specific drug."

"Right, too many variables would make it hard to confirm

anything. But, Bright Stones is a fairly new Enhanced drug. New evidence suggests France is the drug's country of origin. The first cases of Bright Stones overdoses were registered there, and it is currently the country most affected by it. What connects the victims is the language they last spoke at the parties."

Alyssa put a victim ID chart in front of James. The data shown came from translator chips. It detailed each victim's native language and when each chip interfaced with another in order to translate.

"Are you using translator chips' data?" James leaned to take a better look at the report, casting a hulking shadow over the long desk's surface. "Why?"

"Translator chips almost eliminate the need to learn any other languages because we all use them. The funny thing about them, though, is that native speakers can tell when the chip's translating the speech of someone else. The chips haven't yet managed to make it sound natural."

"Huh, that's true. I guess I've never thought about it."

"Most people don't. We're used to it. But in crime rings, this has become a way to identify outsiders. That's why you gotta be a linguist if you want to go on undercover missions."

"Or else you stand out."

"Right."

James continued reading the translator chip report. "Why are these timestamps highlighted?"

"All the victims spoke French with a particular person at the party. These are the times the victims' chips linked with this woman over here." Alyssa pointed at a name on the list of witnesses. "Abrielle Cartier. I looked her up and, in the UK, she has no criminal record."

"But elsewhere?"

"She has a couple of regular drug-related antecedents.

Mostly possession and alleged distribution, but perhaps she's moved to Enhanced drugs. She could be a suspect, a lead."

"Look at you!" James smiled at her with widened eyes. "Alyssa, this is great. What comes next?"

"If I was actually leading the investigation? First, I'd order a full background check on Cartier. If that matched the details of the case, maybe I'd initiate an undercover mission."

"I meant, what do you actually plan to do with this?"

Like a candle that had been blown out, Alyssa felt her warmth leave her. Putting the pieces together for this case was a pastime for her. Just a way to keep her investigative muscle trained. Or so she told herself every time she looked at the reports. Had she been trying to do something else all this time? She could feel James watching her, egging her on to do something more with this information.

"There's nothing I can do about it anymore." Alyssa picked up the case records and closed the folder. "I'm not even supposed to be looking at these. You know that."

"I do," James said. "But I still think you should do something about it. When you first showed me these cases, there were hardly any leads. And now, there's extensive research here to support your new theory."

"Yes, there is."

"Maybe even enough to appeal your exit assessment for the Enhanced Narcotics."

A quick shot of pain in her chest reminded her of how the Enhanced Narcotics Division turned her away right after she graduated from the Academy. The chances of pursuing the career she'd been groomed for were lower than slim. Enhanced Narcotics made it clear they weren't interested, and they were not the only ones. The other divisions at Clover's UK branch needed just one look at her permanent file to dismiss her. The only place left for her was overseas with the Special Response Units.

James took her silence as a cue to continue talking. "Look, I think—"

"That I have a lot of potential? That I should fight to prove myself and get out of this Records Room?"

"Yes, because you're Enhanced! Just like me and every cadet in our division. Enhanced soldiers belong out there, in field missions."

"I know, you've said that before."

"You know what else I've said before? Your talents are wasted in this room. In this Unit, even."

Alyssa scoffed. Talents came naturally. The powers the Enhancement Process gave her, not so much. They came from her father's signature allowing the medical trials when she was a child. "These powers aren't talents."

James gave her one of his mentoring looks. His golden eyes stood out like two harvest moons in the dark umber of his face. "You know what I mean. You're trained for underground work. You speak four languages. You were groomed for the Enhanced Task Forces."

"I appreciate the input, James." She shoved the folder back in its hiding spot. "But I lost that opportunity. Now I have to make new ones over here."

"Is that why you keep working overtime?"

Alyssa gave him a tight-lipped smile. She never planned to be a part of the Special Response Units. With all her training from the Academy dedicated to a different career path, she now needed to spend all her time adjusting to her new line of work. "I'm just trying to make a good impression."

James chuckled. "There are other ways to do that, you know? I can put in a good word with Commander Fox; he can finally send you on field missions with Robin and me."

A pang of panic raised in the back of her head. Field missions meant more opportunities to use her abilities. Alyssa wasn't ready for that, not after the last time she used them. "No." Her voice came out sharper than she intended.

She stood up from her desk and gathered her things into her bag. She gave James a smile, trying to make up for her sharp tone. "I appreciate the sentiment, James, really. But I prefer to do things my way."

James gave her a look as if analyzing her response. "So what's the plan, Alyssa? You can't stay in Records forever."

Alyssa glanced at James from the corner of her eye. "I just want to keep my head down. If I don't ruffle any more feathers in the company, maybe I can keep this job. Start my career on my own terms." And those terms included not touching the raw life force that lived inside her. If she never used her powers again, it would be too soon.

"I think..." He fished for words. "I think it's too late to have this conversation."

"It's too late for my career?" she asked, fear gripping her chest.

"I mean, it's past midnight." James pointed at the numbers on the wall behind them. "We both should go home."

She couldn't contain a bittersweet smirk.

"I'm not giving up on this." James picked up her jacket, almost left behind, and extended it to her. "You should know that already."

Alyssa gave a dry chuckle. "Right."

The blaring of the telecom woke her up. Alyssa opened her eyes. The darkness of her living room clothed her, inviting her to go back to sleep. She forced herself to sit up with a grunt. Her stiff neck complained from her dozing off on the couch. The telecom blared a second time. As she walked to the hall wall to check her messages, she rubbed her eyes and pushed down her red coils, attempting to tame them.

Incoming message from Clover's Special Response Unit Division. The screen read. *Message received at 1:57 am.* She had only slept for about an hour.

Cursing her enthusiasm to work overtime, she continued reading.

New Graysons' Police Department sent a Code 8 at 1:32am. Still groggy, Alyssa's mind stretched to decode the message. She'd received a list of local law enforcement codes when she arrived at Clover's US branch. Code 8. Request for backup.

She leaned forward, focusing on the rest of the message.

Clover Technicians confirmed the presence of a possible Genetically Enhanced Entity (GENE) in the area. Suspect is hostile. Delta Unit is on call. All members report to the assigned Tactical Room immediately.

Her stomach did a somersault. The Delta Unit was hers, but why was she being called in? James and Robin were always the ones responding to calls. She'd never been in the field, much less against a hostile GENE.

A couple of deep breaths later, she remembered her Unit's Average Response Time was being monitored. The longer she took to report to Clover's Tactical Floor, the more points they would get docked.

Alyssa rushed into her tactical gear and out the door. So much for keeping her head down.

MIGUEL_

S *woosh.*

The white and blue-clad figure leaped from one rooftop to the next. Below, the city's former downtown was now a crumbled ruin. Modern apartment buildings, cozy coffee shops, and once upscale offices were replaced by heaps of destruction. In the middle of the gray and dusty scene stood a nine-foot-tall creature garbed in yellow-and-black armor. The shine from the battle garment suggested it had been forged thousands of light-years away. It also identified its wearer as the captain of the fleet of ships responsible for the attacks—the attacks that almost wiped the city of Mount Lycan from existence.

"Zetslen!" The figure in blue jumped down to meet his nemesis. "Your path of destruction and terror ends here!"

The creature turned its head, an intrigued look peering through its elaborate helmet. "Well, if it isn't Earth's last defender. I was sure you had gone down with the others."

The hero tightened his fists, the memory of his fallen comrades urging him to fight, stand up to evil.

"Think again, creature! As long as I'm standing, Earth will

have a protector." The blue hero prepared for battle. "With the power of the seven seas and the vigor of Earth's core, I will stop you. I am the guardian of the blue planet this side of the Milky Way. I am the Terra Ranger."

The creature bent backward with a guttural laugh, a sound of unnatural, mechanical scratching. "You've come to stop me? Very well. I'll allow you a warrior's death."

Zetslen took a fighting stance, towering over Terra like a massive monolith in black-and-yellow colors. "What's it going to be, hero?"

"Miguel?" A faraway voice called to him.

Miguel lifted his eyes from his tablet. He'd been reading the colorful panels of what was perhaps the most epic battle yet in the *Rangers of Earth* series.

A nurse stood at the other end of the waiting room. "Doctor Sharp will be ready to see you in just a moment."

Miguel thanked her and made his way to the examination room. Terra, the battle for Earth's destiny, and all the other colorful superheroes would have to wait.

The doctor's office looked more like an overly sanitized closet. There was a desk, a metal table cornered against the bleached white walls, and a sad, gray curtain meant to provide a sense of privacy.

The nurse left him with instructions to sign the patient log and get changed. Miguel walked to the patient log on the desk and found his name. He scribbled a signature and added his date of birth next to it. November 22. He'd turn thirteen in just four more days.

The door closed behind the nurse, and Miguel slipped behind the gray curtain. He stripped off his pants and took a paper robe from the table. He checked twice that no one was coming before jumping out of his underwear and into the paper robe. He folded his clothes on the table, but they still ended up a messy pile of soft squares.

A knock on the door announced Doctor Jessica Sharp's entrance. Her messy ponytail, ashy skin, and dark marks under her olive eyes suggested she'd been up late working. She offered him a small hand. "Good afternoon, Mister De Santos."

Miguel smiled. The sound of his last name on the doctor's lips made him feel extra official. He shook her hand with practiced confidence. "Hi."

"How are we doing today?" The doctor launched into her daily script, her voice dry and robotic.

Miguel sat on the cold metal table. "I'm okay, thanks."

The doctor grabbed a clipboard holding her notes. The wooden board had a red logo on the back. A red four-leaf clover, with a DNA helix in place of a stem. "No headaches, nausea, or unexplained fatigue?"

"No."

"And Mister De Santos, have we experienced any loss of appetite, sudden blindness, dry mouth, dry skin, rashes, heart acceleration, flashes of sudden pain, nose or eye bleeding?"

Miguel shook his head, and the doctor leaned forward to swab the inside of his mouth.

"How about recurrent nightmares, hallucinations, a sense of being followed, hand sweating, or spontaneous crying?"

"Nope."

She flashed a light in his eyes. He blinked tears away twice. The cold metal of a stethoscope on his chest sent a chill down his back.

"I have good news, then." Doctor Sharp let the stethoscope rest around her neck. "Since none of the secondary effects of the Enhancement Process have manifested, we can move on to the next phase."

Miguel smiled back, a little proud of the results. He watched the doctor return to her desk.

"To close Phase One, we'll do more blood work and move on to Phase Two next week." The doctor paused to take notes on her tablet. "I expect that we'll start seeing obvious signs of mutations soon after."

"And then no more radiation sessions, right?" The words slipped out before he could catch them. He wished he'd kept both the question and the added tone of hopefulness to himself.

Doctor Sharp lifted her eyes and took off her glasses with her free hand. "I'm afraid not. The sessions will continue as they are right now. We're just adding extra blood work and closer monitoring."

The answer left him with a pit in his stomach. It was a shock to him to realize just how much he'd hoped for the radiation sessions to be over.

The doctor must have realized that too, because she offered him a sympathetic smile. "Let's adjourn to the radiation room. The sooner we get in there, the sooner we get it over with, okay?"

Miguel nodded, preparing himself for what was to come. What was to come today, next week, the one after that, and many more after.

Two heavy metal doors hid away the radiation lab. Miguel suspected there was something special about the doors that kept the radiation inside. He followed the Enhancement team through the first door and into the prep area. Medical and engineering staff got into their hazmat suits while Miguel stepped into the decontaminating shower. Warm steam whispered over his skin, washing bacteria away.

The second door opened with a loud hum. Cold seeped out from the lab, licking at Miguel's naked feet. He followed the doctors in their bulky suits, wearing his paper robe and nothing else.

The radiation room still took his breath away. Miguel walked around the radiation lab, thinking how different it was from what he had originally pictured it. He thought it should have been just another sterile hospital lab. But the room's earthy colored walls and the dull, lilac light coming from the artificial skylight just reminded him of a newly discovered cave somewhere in the Sahara. Nausea stirred deep in his stomach when his eyes focused on the black vault sitting in the middle of the room. The radiation chamber stretched from floor to ceiling, an eerie monolith.

Miguel reminded himself how scared he'd been when he left the *Nuestra Señora de la Paz* Youth Refugee Center. He told himself it was high time he started being brave. He'd march into that radiation chamber and endure the pain just like the heroes in his comics. Terra wasn't afraid when he fought off a hoard of aliens all by himself, or when the space army tortured him. He would be brave this time. If he wasn't, how could he ever become a hero like Terra and the other Rangers?

The Enhancement team rushed past him to their workstations. The sound of people of science at work did nothing to break his focus on the chamber. He stared at the black vault like a cowboy ready to draw at high noon.

The team of engineers clicked away at their computers. Electric whirring and the sound of steam escaping heavy machinery inundated the room. The radiation chamber awoke with the sound of metal scratching. An unnatural, mechanical, guttural laugh.

Miguel's heart jumped to his throat, and his lower lip trembled. He looked away, angry at himself. After almost a hundred visits to the Enhancements Lab, he still trembled with fear at the threshold.

What's it going to be, hero?

Miguel forced the fear down. He made it into a tiny ball and swallowed it. He had to remember what was important. More important than his Clover Academy Scholarship. More important than his green card or refugee status. Even more so than the citizenship status Commander Fox was working on getting him. Enhancements meant superpowers. Nothing else mattered.

"We're ready for you, Mister De Santos." Doctor Sharp's voice drifted in, muffled from behind her hazmat mask.

Miguel nodded and entered the radiation chamber. The door of the chamber closed with a loud crack behind him. Miguel stood in the dark chamber, wearing nothing but the hammer of his heart. A yellow light turned on above him. The session would start when that light turned green.

A sharp breath in later, he positioned himself against the back wall of the machine. Needles punctured his back along the spine. He ground his teeth as an abrasive pain ran through him. The yellow light in the chamber flashed at intervals, counting down. The drum of his heart boomed stronger than before, loud in its own chamber of fleshy walls, echoing his desire to scream. In the last seconds before the light turned green, Miguel promised himself he wouldn't cry. This time, he would be strong. A cold, oily substance injected into his body. He pushed the pain away and closed his eyes. Behind the darkness of his eyelids, there was nothing. No radiation chamber, no doctors, no Enhancements. He took deep breaths inside the darkness surrounding him.

What's it going to be, hero?

Breath in, then out. In and out. In. Out.

Behind the darkness of his eyelids, there was something. A warm light enveloped him, lifted him up, and delivered him to a dirt road. The ground below was wet with scattered rain under his naked feet. The air carried a heavy sea mist along with the smells of salt and clay. Up the dirt road, a small house with a chicken coop posed as if for a greeting card. The makeshift improvements made it look like a collage of family homes in the slums of a seashore city. Miguel caught a whiff of roasted tomatoes and peppers. Under the sound of the light showers falling over aluminum roofs, he heard the voice of a woman. The song she sang carried an earthy tune that spoke about freedom and revolution. It called out to the beaten-down, the heartbroken, and the invisible.

The woman's song drowned without notice by a strenuous roar. Miguel couldn't place the sound. Was it the cry of a train's locomotion? No. It was a military convoy.

Miguel opened his eyes and found the lights of the chamber flickering green and yellow as he was bombarded with radiation. The pain in his chest was so strong he forgot the pain in his back. A single tear fell from his eyelash. Miguel knew he'd failed. Just like he had in every session before.

The smell of rubbing alcohol burned his nostrils. The incessant beeping of the machines in the Recovery Hall gave him a thumping headache. He sat up to avoid putting pressure on his back, sharp prickles running up his spine.

A nurse with curly, dark hair worked next to him as he sipped on a peach-colored electrolyte drink. She gave him an IV and connected him to a machine that would soon pump him full of the chemicals his frail body needed after such an extreme radiation session.

"All done, sweetheart. You'll feel like new in a few

minutes." The nurse motioned to the table next to him and grabbed his tablet. "Why don't you read while we wait?"

Miguel stared at the device. Brown, glassy eyes stared back at him from the dark smudged screen. He shook his head. Stories of extraordinary and brave people would only remind him of how he failed to be strong.

"No, thanks." The nurse frowned at his lack of enthusiasm for heroes in color-coded uniforms. "My head hurts," he managed.

"I can also turn on the TV if you'd like."

"I'm okay, thanks."

"All right, then. I'll be at my desk; holler if you need anything."

Miguel laid down on his side. He closed his eyes, an empty feeling in his chest. He felt like a drifting balloon tied to a patio chair, abandoned among the remains of a birthday party.

He squeezed his eyes tight, trying to force his thoughts away. Away from the idea of going inside the radiation chamber again. Away from the crisp image of the house with the chicken coop that burned so intensely in the back of his mind.

CRIMSON_

W ithin fifteen minutes of leaving her apartment, Alyssa arrived at the Clover building. After passing through security, she ran to the lobby elevators. She fumbled to retrieve her badge, which kept catching in her flapping jacket. She swiped her Level Three clearance badge, and an elevator dinged for her.

An almost-human female voice greeted her. "Welcome, Alyssa Dietrich, AKA Crimson Thunder."

"Twelve, please."

The elevator hummed and rose, beeping with every passing floor. Alyssa leaned against the back of the elevator to catch her breath. Was it the run that made her heart hammer like that? Or the anticipation?

"Twelfth floor, Tactical Rooms." The elevator doors opened.

Alyssa rushed past a hall of doors and looked for the one that read "Delta" on a copper plaque. She had only been in that room once before, upon her arrival to the US branch. With Clover being the international leader in the field of Defense Research, she expected the Deltas would have more resources at their disposal. No such luck.

The lack of high-tech equipment made the Delta Tactical Room look more like a circular classroom. No electronic walls displaying maps and satellite-calculated routes. No intercoms or tactical military devices. They had three half-moon desks lining the walls and a projector.

She found James and Robin sitting at their neighboring work stations, already dressed in their field uniforms. No sight of Commander Fox or his assistant.

"Jesus, Crimson. Did you get run over on your way over? You look awful." Robin, the second-in-command for her Unit, removed a strand of her silvery hair from her face with a delicate swipe of her hand.

"Leave her alone, Robin. It's her first time on call."

Alyssa plopped at the third desk next to James. "Have you been waiting long?"

"Not really, but I suspect we're going to."

James and Robin exchanged a complicit look.

"Paperwork?"

"Yeah." James put a hand to his mouth and covered a yawn he'd fail to suppress. "The commander has to deal with some extra red tape to get us briefing information. He's getting clearance on police footage now."

"It happens more often than not. It's his only fashionable trait." Robin winked, but Alyssa didn't miss her cynical tone.

James shook his head. "He'll be here any minute now."

"Okay." Alyssa's stomach went to knots, led by uncertainty. "What do we know so far?"

"Just what was in our telecoms. Some Enhanced asshole is making a mess downtown."

Enhanced. That word told her so little about the job she was meant to do. It didn't tell her what class of Enhancement the suspect had. Didn't help her plan for an encounter.

Worse yet, it didn't let her plan for the prospect of using her powers.

"What's the matter?" Robin broke her trance. "First-time jitters?"

"I guess so. I wasn't exactly expecting to be called."

James grimaced. "It had to happen sometime."

Alyssa raised her eyebrows. Had he actually gone to Fox to get her into field missions? "Did you—?"

"No." James put his hands up. "This is all Commander Fox."

Her mouth felt dry. If Fox was calling the whole Unit in, he might need all hands on deck. He might even grant them all GENE clearance and expect her to use her powers.

"Oh, come on." Robin smirked as if it were all a strange joke. "You didn't think you could hide in Records forever, did you?"

"Well, no." Alyssa sighed. Special Response Units were teams of GENEs fighting other GENEs. Rogue ones. From the start, she knew her assignment to the Records Room was only temporary. Reading old Delta reports was only delaying the inevitable. "It's just... We have no idea what the target's abilities look like. If there is no information about the GENE class, how can we be prepared?"

"That's why we get the police footage."

"And if that is not enough?"

James gave her one of his relaxed smiles. "Very unlikely. Commander Fox has a lot of experience with rogue GENEs, and he keeps an eye on any new Classes." Her face must've shown how unconvinced she felt because he continued. "You know, he used to be in the Enhanced Task Forces back in his day. There's nothing the guy hasn't tackled before. Besides—" James gestured to the room around them "—we have the best equipment we could possibly need here. Cutting edge stuff."

The Deltas joined in a bitter laugh.

The optimism and humor of her teammates were contagious. The knot in her stomach subsided, but worry still lurked in the back of her mind.

"It'll be fine, Crimson." Robin's voice was smooth and reassuring. "The suspect will probably be a Transhuman Class mook with super strength. Very common."

"Hey! I resent that." James flexed an arm, showing off a gigantic bicep. "We Transhumans get the job done better than anyone."

"Your GENE Class is just easier to make," Robin added with a sharp smirk.

"Whatever." James rolled his eyes but still snickered. "There's beauty in simplicity. No need for fancy blood or sparkly light shows, like you two." He pointed at Robin and Alyssa in turn.

Alyssa could not contain a snicker at his expense. "How sensitive."

"The Adamant Tiger, everyone," Robin said as a ringmaster would. "The unbreakable body with the softest feelings."

The doors opened with a wham, wiping Alyssa's smile off her face. The Deltas rose in full military salutation.

Through the double doors marched Commander Millard Fox in shiny shoes, pressed uniform, clean-shaven face, and a focused golden gaze that completed his attire. His assistant, Honey Graf, followed suit. Her heels made a statement as she walked to the projector.

The commander walked past them, jumping straight to the briefing. "Look alive, people. We've got a lot of work to do."

The lights in the room went out. Blurry images projected on the white wall at the opposite end of the Tactical Room.

"We have what looks like a terrorist attack in our hands. We're waiting to hear on any casualties, but there have been at least eighteen people hurt." Fox continued talking as his assistant adjusted the projector. "Civilians reported an attack on patrons and security personnel inside the Blue Flamingo Club in the Arts District. Our suspect could be using Enhanced weaponry. Or he could be Enhanced, but not by us. At any rate, his attack on the public falls under our jurisdiction." The Commander grabbed the clicker for the projector from his pocket. "He's endangered the GENE Secrecy."

The projector kicked into gear with the wiring of cooling fans. Night lights and modern architecture flashed on the white wall. People walked from one end of the street strip in nightlife attire. The white stone building that was New Graysons' City Hall glimmered in the distance. Alyssa recognized the Arts District's High Street, not sure what she was supposed to be looking at.

"This is John Doe 0397." Fox clicked to a close-up.

A scrawny guy with ashy blond hair was now the focus of the next picture. He wore run-down military fatigues and a dirty olive jacket that was way too big for him. The image made Alyssa think of a painting. Nothing like the colorful, safe art she could find at museums nowadays. This was like the kind of painting one would see a starving artist trying to sell on a street corner. One that made a statement against society.

Robin scoffed. "Him? He's our alleged terrorist?"

Alyssa had to agree with Robin. At first glance, 0397 looked like some poor guy down on his luck.

"I thought the same thing when I first saw him. But then law enforcement delivered this footage taken right outside the Blue Flamingo." Fox moved to the next slide and clicked on a video file.

Thirty-five seconds of confusion played on the screen. The microphones in the police car picked up the cry of the sirens and what sounded like civilian commotion. Had a car caught on fire in the distance? The video footage zeroed in on their suspect. He'd lost the jacket and stood in the middle of the street. If Commander Fox hadn't identified him as the suspect, she would have thought this was a completely different person. His stance was different, and his eyes promised violence. Did he have a prosthesis in place of one of his arms? Or was that part of a military-grade exoskeleton suit? The police car approached him. 0397 turned to look at the police car and disappeared from the camera's view. An eye blink later, a loud bang rattled the vehicle's camera.

Alyssa's stomach did a somersault. Had they run him over?

'Did you see that?!' the driver said to his partner. 'He's on top of us!'

'Call it in!'

One of the cops scrambled out of the car while the other one grabbed the radio. 'Three David Three. Dispatch, do you copy?'

'On the ground, now!' the cop on the street yelled.

'Come in, Three David Three.'

'This is a Code 8 from the Arts District...'

A gun fired once. Twice. Three times. The camera caught a visual of 0397 again. He disarmed the cop in two moves and crushed the gun in a silvery hand.

The video stopped, the image frozen on that silvery grip crushing the gun.

Silence settled in the room.

"What is that?" Alyssa heard James ask behind her.

"This is 0397's weapon of choice," Fox answered. "Looks like an advanced exoskeleton suit or an Enhanced prosthesis."

"I've never seen anything like it."

Fox turned to his Unit, the image on the projector partially reflecting on the medals pinned to his chest. "Neither have I."

TIGER_

Tension rose to James' temples. How was it possible that Fox didn't know the suspect's abilities?

All the resources the company poured into this Special Response Units went toward eliminating threats that could expose the existence of GENEs to the public. Commander Fox had been working under this division for over a decade. If anyone knew about any new variations, it would be one of the four Unit commanders. And yet, this was different. Fox could not give them any insight into the suspect's GENE class, weaknesses, or strengths.

James' job was to devise a strategy to protect the GENE Secrecy and the public from Enhanced threats. Without Fox's knowledge, he was lost. His Unit would be expecting orders from him.

The projector turned off, and the lights in the tactical room came back on, and Fox started talking so fast that James struggled to process his words.

"0397 was reported injured after his encounter with the police. He was last seen running towards the corner of Main and 7th," Fox said. "Track him down. Bring him in. Alive. You'll get two Omega bodies to support you. Agent Maloney and Bridges are waiting at the garage with two untagged vehicles."

"Sir," Robin's voice drifted in. "Only two? That isn't even a full non-Enhanced Unit."

"They are the only ones I could get you on such short notice. Now go. This is still an emergency, even if the rest of the company decides to forget that. Get your tactical kits from Honey on your way out."

The weight of his three hundred pounds fell heavy on James' shoulders as he stood up from his chair. On their way out, he noticed Alyssa take her first-ever tactical kit. She had graduated from the Clover Academy just last spring. She was only eighteen years old. Apprehension grew in his chest—her first time in the field would be messy. He'd assured her Fox would know what to do. What if something happened to her?

He needed to get a hold of himself. Alyssa was green but capable. He and Fox picked her from a select handful of recruits because of her qualifications.

"Tiger?" Commander Fox called him before he could make his way out.

"Sir."

"I suspect I don't need to tell you how important this mission is. Still, a word of caution never hurt anyone. This case will need special attention. If we are dealing with a new GENE class, it could be coming from another country, looking to send a message." Fox's golden gaze had the sharpness of a chess grandmaster. "We're only getting this case because Units Alpha, Beta, and Gamma are already on call. This is the first GENE case our Unit has taken in a long while. The outcome of this mission might determine whether this will be our last."

A heavy sigh got stuck in James' chest. His Unit had been serving as the departments' benchwarmers for longer than he'd liked to admit. After Clover's Military Department demanded that all units needed to have at least three members, the Deltas were moved to the back burner. Considered incomplete, they'd been only taking on miscellaneous cases no one else would.

"The Department Directors have made it very clear." Commander Fox's stern face gave nothing away. "They've been looking for excuses to disband our Unit for months. I need our Unit strong out there, Tiger. Stronger than ever."

James' posture grew rigid. Fox was right—he needed to focus. "Yes, sir."

With a military salute, the commander dismissed him. James picked up his tactical kit and headed out of the room.

This is our chance, he thought as he pulled his electronic tablet with his briefing notes. *If we succeed, we can finally rise above our station. We could finally stop worrying about the company disbanding our Unit on a whim. But if we fail?*

He thanked Honey and followed the rest of his Unit out of the room.

"Such short notice—" Robin said next to him in a mocking tone while they walked through the halls. "Such bullshit. We're the Fixed Foxes, and everyone knows it."

James acknowledged her comment with a grunt as he read. He didn't miss the added bitterness in Robin's tone. The other three units in their division called them the Fixed Foxes to their backs. As much as James preferred to ignore the moniker, it served as a reminder of the indifference they faced. James wasn't sure what the company disliked about his commander. None of the other commanders were GENEs, and maybe the others disliked an Enhanced person so high up in the food chain.

There were whispers here and there about something called the Enhanced People's Rights Movement—maybe Fox was suspected to be involved with it. Whatever it was that they disliked about Fox, it meant all the resources at their disposal were nothing but scraps.

"So, what's the plan?" Alyssa's question came with an added tone of uneasiness.

"Yes, oh wise leader, brief us." Robin had put her long silvery hair into a high ponytail. The syringe vial at her hip caught the light. Antidote for her venom. If they needed the target alive, they all had one in their tactical kits. He made a mental note to double-check for his.

James forced his thoughts back to the case. Strategies and plans churned in the back of his mind as he read. "Our target was last seen fleeing east. From the Arts District, he could have gone either closer to City Hall or towards the Development District."

"What are you thinking?" Robin asked as she pressed the down button three times in a row when they reached the elevator. "Could he be planning another attack?"

James shook his head. "The police reported him hurt. He'll be looking for a place to heal. The parks around City Hall or the abandoned warehouses in the Development District would provide the most shelter."

The elevator dinged for them.

"We only have two vehicles to mobilize, and we don't have enough reinforcements for everyone to have back up."

Robin cursed under her breath as they climbed into the elevator. "Ridiculous."

"We'll have to make it work," James continued, knowing there was no time to agree with Robin. "If we split up the Unit in three, we get to cover more ground. Alyssa, I'll send you to the City Hall area. Take our Omega forces and brief them on the way."

Alyssa nodded. "Understood."

James turned to his second-in-command. "Robin, you'll go

to the Development District. I'll touch base with law enforcement at the scene and move from there."

The elevator dinged once they reached the lower levels of the Clover Building. Dimness cloaked the wide garage, and cold night air blew inside, like a winter breeze entering a cave. They found their support waiting for them next to two untagged Jeeps. Both soldiers donned the black Clover uniform with the red cap that identified them as Omega support elements. On an ideal day, each Delta member would have received a vehicle plus two soldiers for individual backup.

"Well, kids." Robin clicked her tongue and raised an eyebrow. "Time to make it work."

She stepped out of the elevator first, her confident steps echoing as she approached their elements. "All right, listen up!" Robin clapped her hands, the sound muffled by her gloves. "This is the Delta Unit, mission code 77-84, AKA The Blue Flamingo Incident. Unit Leader on duty, Adamant Tiger. Second, Silver Komodo. Third, Crimson Thunder." Robin pointed at James, herself, and Alyssa. "You will be Omega One, and you Omega Two."

James continued where Robin had left off. "Omega One and Two, you're with Crimson. Comb the northeast area. I want all the parks around City Hall searched. Komodo, you're on rooftop duty. I want sharp eyes closer to the Development District. I'll take the groundwork from the crime scene. Report back to HQ if you find anything. We want the target alive. Move out!"

"You heard him," Robin said. "Let's go, people!"

The Unit dispersed into action. James climbed into the passenger's side of one of the untagged Jeeps, Robin in the driver's seat. The engine roared awake. James let out a loud sigh.

"You good?" Robin asked, eyes on the road.

"I'm fine," James lied. "Why do you ask?"

"I saw your face fall when Fox said this is some sort of new freak he hasn't seen before. You wanted to order Alyssa to stay behind." Robin took a left at the end of the street. "I'm surprised you didn't."

Robin knew him well. "It's not up to me," James answered. Fox had made himself clear. "This isn't some security detail mission or a low profile international escort. This is the chance we've been waiting for. A case this big will force the company to look at us, and it has to see all of us as a complete unit."

Robin looked surprised. "Good."

The silence between them lasted a heartbeat.

"James, if we fail—"

"We can't." James glanced out the window. A full moon rested at the highest point in the night sky, dark clouds threatening to swallow it up. "There's a lot riding on this."

Robin dropped him off right outside The Blue Flamingo Club. The flames from a car licked high, black smoke lifting like a menacing cloud as firefighters tried to put it out to no avail. How had that fire started? Ambulances and cop cars were scattered on either side of Main Street. In the distance, the cry of a second fire truck announced its arrival. The victims of the Blue Flamingo Incident sat on the sidewalks with paramedic-issued blankets over their shoulders. Some spoke to law enforcement, some were tended to by paramedics, and others were left alone to stare at the flames. The blood orange lights flickered on their dirt-and sweat-stained faces, accentuating every bit of their numbed expressions.

James' face grew hard as stone. He forced himself to focus on the mission. A cop to his right had just finished interviewing a witness. James approached him, determined to get answers.

"Clover Unit on call." He flashed his Clover Military badge

in front of him. "Spare a moment, officer?"

With cold regard, the policeman contemplated his badge. The man looked up at him. The look on his face made James feel massive but insufficient; it reminded James of looking up at the Thanksgiving floats as a child and thinking, *Is that all?*

The officer glanced behind James, maybe hoping to glimpse the rest of the parade. "Don't tell me they only sent you."

The policeman's demeanor didn't surprise James. As far as this man was concerned, James was just a regular man working under Clover's private army—just some guy who didn't make it in the real armed forces. And he was there to take the case away from his people.

"We have a full Unit checking the perimeter. I'm just here to touch base with you guys."

"Good. I don't care how big you are. You couldn't've taken that freak on your own."

"What do you know of the suspect?" James ignored the cop's snideness. "Did anyone see where he went?"

"We have conflicting reports." The cop shrugged. "Witnesses saw the suspect flee west. My money's on the parking garages at Main and Fifth. I could let you talk to some folks, but they are more concerned with what the guy could do than where he went." He looked at James sideways and lowered his voice. "The things people are saying."

James' stomach went cold. If he was going to have a chance to report on any larger risks to the GENE secrecy, this was it. "What are people saying?"

"Some witnesses say it was just a guy with guns. You know, a typical shooting." The cop took a deep breath as if bracing himself to try to wrap his head around the whole incident. "Some others are talking crazy."

"What kind of crazy?"

"*Secret Soldier* kind of stuff. You know, superpowers and

all."

The cold in his stomach went all the way to his feet—he knew the movie. An army guy got altered by the government with alien technology. It was a fantasy verging too close to reality for Clover's comfort. Information like this could not be spread out. Civilians were already wary of using post-war technology for medicine and energy supplies. To find out governments around the world were using it to experiment on soldiers would be catastrophic. If the truth about what happened at the Blue Flamingo got out, Clover would have to control the press and silence any witnesses by any means necessary. It was the part of his job James didn't like to think about.

"On the other hand, these people were having fun. The club was dark. Some of them are saying a fight broke out inside and that the guy had just a knife." The cop paused as if trying to weigh in what was possible and what wasn't. "We don't know what to think."

James gave him a reassuring smile, hating himself for what he was about to say. "No wonder. These new drugs are pretty freaky."

"Drugs?"

"Yeah, some kind of Enhanced PCP. Temporarily ups your strength and agility. Melts your brain." James waved a dismissive hand in front of him. "You know, the usual."

"Oh."

"You didn't really think the guy had superpowers, right? That's impossible."

"No, no. Of course not."

James could see the doubt and bewilderment diminish in the cop's eyes. He told himself that was enough to keep everyone out of trouble. He shook hands with the police officer and made his way to Fifth Street, the taste of lies and ashes heavy in his mouth.

MIGUEL_

Cool sand against his skin told him he was at the beach even before he opened his eyes. The taste of salt in the air and the cry of waves breaking ashore brought him back to a beach he knew. He hung tight to those sensations, afraid to open his eyes and find himself elsewhere. Memories played behind his closed eyelids.

Miguel was back in San Gerónimo. He ran under a Chilean sky painted in tones of orange and purple. A Sunday afternoon stretched before him. A soccer ball shuffled at his feet while his siblings chased after him. Sun-kissed skin glistened with sweat, and naked toes dug into moist sand. His side hurt from laughter. He was home.

Eyes closed, Miguel grabbed a handful of sand. His heart sank. It was wrong—like fine dust, not San Gerónimo's mineral-rich sand. The only way he could be back in San Gerónimo was if this was a dream. The Russians with their tanks and their oil rig made sure of that. He lived in New Graysons now, with its gray skies and its tall, cold buildings. Clover was home now.

But then, Miguel thought as he felt the leftover sand on his fingers, *where is this?*

He opened his eyes to a starless night sky, paved with water-heavy clouds. He was at a beach, but it wasn't the one from his childhood. How did he end up there? Miguel's mind stretched through sleepy memories. He remembered the distant chatter of nurse gossip and the smell of stale morning coffee. The taste of salty peaches in his mouth reminded him of the Recovery Hall. The last thing he remembered was needing an IV infusion after his radiation session. He must've fallen asleep waiting for the drugs to work on him.

As he sat up, a sharp pain hit his side. The pain extended over his ribs, and he struggled to breathe. He winced, pushing the pain aside as he tried to figure out where he was.

Miguel caught a glimpse of fluorescent jellyfish lining the shoreline. Thousands upon thousands of them lay over the sand, demarcating the border between land and sea. Lying increasingly still, dying. If they'd known what awaited them on the other side of the shoreline, would they have come?

Movement near him caught his attention. Miguel's stomach trembled. He wasn't alone. From the corner of his eye, he saw a girl in a white hospital gown. He turned to get a better look, and his skin crawled. The girl sat close to him, hugging her legs and resting her head on her knees. Her long, silky hair hung over her shoulder, weaved into an intricate braid. Some strands of hair escaped the complex design and floated around her. They seemed to move on their own, like strings of smoke. It looked as if her braid were made of needle-thick shadows. A shadow braid.

The girl sat upright and turned to him. She cocked her head, studying him as if trying to solve something about him.

Miguel opened his mouth to speak, but no sound came out of him.

There was an air of mysticism to Shadow Braid that reminded him of the stories his grandmother used to tell. She'd tell him about the ever-mysterious women who wandered the streets at night. They'd wailed lamentations of their past lives, whisked children up to never be seen again, or disarmed grown men with one terrifying look.

Shadow Braid wasn't wailing, but her piercing gaze made Miguel's heart race with anticipation. She gave him a plastic, painted smile, like a doll's. Almost mechanically, Shadow Braid leaned over to him and touched his side. A stump of pain rushed to him upon contact. Shadow Braid patted the area to find nothing was broken. The touch was soft yet firm, a healer's touch. Miguel wasn't afraid anymore.

"Who are you?" His voice came out like a murmuring echo.

The waves whispered as they broke on the shore.

Shadow Braid looked up at him, her expression blank and hard-to-read. She touched her throat as if she were choking.

It took Miguel a second to figure out what she meant. "You can't speak."

She shook her head, with that neutral expression that seemed to be as learned and practiced as her plastic smiles.

"I guess this means you can't tell me where we are."

The girl in the white gown cocked her head with another painted smile. She pointed up to the skies behind him. Miguel followed her finger, but it wasn't hard to figure out what she was pointing to.

Amongst the clouds, there was what he could only describe as a hole. A closer look revealed the Recovery Hall as he remembered it. If he strained his eyes for long enough, Miguel could see himself back at the Recovery Hall, sleeping, still hooked up to the IV machine. It all reminded him of an issue in *Rangers of Earth*, where the team of superheroes traveled through different planes of existence. Was that hole in the clouds an opening to another dimension?

The side of his head hurt, his brain trying to organize all the questions he had. Ghosts, other dimensions, beaches. He had to be dreaming. The radiation session took a lot out of him, and now he was having an IV-induced dream.

He turned around to find his companion was already making her way to the other side of the beach.

"Wait! Where are you going?" The words came out before he could remember she wouldn't be able to answer.

Thunder cracked behind him with such intensity that it made him jump. Gusts of air pushed the already dark clouds closer together, covering the open space that led to the Recovery Hall. A tropical storm was about to begin, and Shadow Braid was walking away from it. Maybe she knew where to find shelter.

By the time he caught up with Shadow Braid, Miguel had to stop and nurse his hurt side. The pain on his ribs stabbed him every time he exhaled.

"W-where are you going?" he managed while catching his breath.

Shadow Braid turned back and stared at him. The ground trembled beneath them. Behind her, a hole in the sand opened. It looked as if the beach were yawning. Another hole. Was she trying to take him to a different place? Could she really take him to another dimension?

The light of the jellyfish in the sand made Shadow Braid look like a stone statue, her dark eyes urging him to follow.

"I can't." Miguel stared into the void. "This is just a dream."

Lightning and thunder cracked behind them, announcing the start of the storm. Shadow Braid cocked her head, the strands of jet black hair flowing around her like ghostly snakes.

This wasn't a dream.

She extended her hand towards Miguel, but he didn't take it. With his entrails in knots, he turned around, walking towards the storm.

TIGER_

The cold of the parking garage bit at James through the layers of tactical gear and the unnecessary bulletproof vest. Darkness layered onto itself the deeper he walked into the garage's lower levels.

A splash with a wet echo caught James' attention. He flashed the light on his gun over the dark corner. Like a stage light, he illuminated the scurries of yet another rat he'd startled.

James checked the stopwatch on his wrist, the muscles on his back tightening into a knot. He'd spent the last fifteen minutes following that lead and had nothing to show for it. Nothing but rats.

He tapped the radio on his shoulder. "Adamant Tiger to HQ."

"Go ahead, Tiger." Honey's voice resonated in his ear. "Report."

"I'm sweeping a parking garage at Main and Fifth. Police witnesses reported seeing 0397 come this way. What do you have for me?"

"Nothing yet. We're running the facial recognition databases and can't find our target."

James thought he'd misheard her at first. Even if 0397 didn't have a criminal record, he should at least come up in the international civilian database. Unless he didn't have a translator chip.

"We might be dealing with an off-the-grid entity," Honey finished. "We'll keep you in the loop, Tiger."

James rogered that and left the frequency. His radio made a static noise when he turned it off. The sound that followed wasn't its echo. It sounded to him like lamentations of pain.

According to the briefing, 0397 was hurt and on the run, probably lying low. James listened carefully. Maybe 0397 was here after all.

Caution and expectation bumped in his chest as he climbed to level fifteen. A single sepia light bulb illuminated the whole floor, aided only by the glow of a nearby streetlight that filtered in through the garage's balcony. A flash of dirty yellow hair at the far end of the floor told James he wasn't alone.

Suspect 0397 sat leaning against a pillar. He'd torn a piece of his fatigues and held it against his side to stop the bleeding. A smell of burnt flesh and sweat hung in the air.

James hit the red button on his radio, sending a silent alarm to his team. He had the target. Now it was just a matter of not letting him slip away.

He's not going anywhere with that wound.

James pointed his automatic at 0397, his voice booming from the depths of his chest. "Freeze!"

0397 stood up as the gun's light shined over him. Fresh gray eyes stared at James. Primal aggression behind them delivered a warning. James was the hunter stepping into the wounded wolf's lair, and he wasn't welcome.

"I said freeze!" James cocked the gun when 0397 took a step closer to the light.

In person, 0397 looked young. He was younger than James expected, not a day over eighteen if he had to bet. The hollow cheeks and the way the skin wrapped around the kid's bones almost made James drop his weapon. Until he saw it. A slick silver and almost liquid alloy shined over 0397's right arm. The metal extended all the way to the shoulder, ending on a wide plaque just atop his chest.

James felt his mind stretch as he attempted to remember any knowledge of biotechnology. This couldn't be a prosthesis or exoskeleton like Fox said in his briefing. It had an almost too-natural fit over the arm to be a machine.

0397 took another step forward. Was James really going to have to shoot him? Maybe he needed a different approach.

James lowered his weapon a little. "I've seen what you can do. Super strength, increased agility."

0397's gaze darted to him and back to the gun.

"You might be able to take me on." James shrugged. "But you're hurt, and I bet you're tired, too Wouldn't you like to give this up?"

0397 shook like a spring that had been under pressure for a second too long. He kept looking around him, looking for a way out.

"Let's relax for a second, huh?" James continued. He compromised, completely lowering his gun. "Just get down, and I'll take you in. We'll get you out of the cold, put some warm food in you, and someone can take a look at that wound you have going on over there. How 'bout it?"

The confusion on 0397's face reminded James of what life was like before translator chips existed. Was 0397 not understanding his words? James took a step closer but realized it was the wrong move a second too late.

Like a snarling animal, 0397 lurched forward, faster than James would have expected. James lifted his gun and squeezed the trigger. Just as the bullet left the barrel, 0397 crushed the gun, concealing the shot in a silver grip.

James tossed the gun behind him and put some distance between them. Next thing he knew, 0397 drew his hand back, just like a knife thrower. Something twinkled with a soft blue light between his fingers. James covered his face with a thick forearm when he saw the weapons fly towards him.

Clank.

Whatever 0397 threw at him bounced right off. His invulnerable skin protected him. James peered at the weapons in 0397's hand. They were four dagger-sized disks, a cyan light shining around them. The glow looked like those plasma knives used to cut through steel and to cauterize wounds on the battlefield. Plasma disks.

When he looked back at his opponent, he found a look of bewilderment he wasn't expecting. 0397 had clearly never seen something his disks couldn't cut through. James gave him a little smile, proud of his own abilities.

0397 rushed at him again. He connected military-grade punches with the speed and grace of a martial artist. James waited for an opening to try to get his opponent in a hold. No luck. He couldn't keep up. In fights with speedsters, he only had his boulder-like defense.

After several attempts to overpower each other, 0397 jumped back. He panted, looking flushed and feverish. He held his side, wincing. If James didn't know better, he'd say there was some internal bleeding in that wound.

"Of course you're tired," James heard himself say with the same tone he had used to train new recruits years ago. "You fight like you're running out of time. No strategy, no finesse. Raw force isn't going to take you anywhere. Time to give it up, kid."

0397 gave him another confused yet annoyed look. He whipped his arm to the side; a long and menacing blade came out from his forearm.

"You won't give up, will you?" James shook his head and decided to stop playing defense.

James shuffled into the next bout like a boxer into the ring. 0397 dashed his punches, making James' arms feel like they weighed a ton. James switched gears, hoping to tackle 0397 this time. The kid jumped out of his reach, and in midair, the blade coming from his forearm connected with the nape of James' neck. James heard a switch click somewhere, and the blade started to vibrate.

A hot pain invaded his neck. Sparks flew in the air as the sound of metal scraping metal screeched across the parking garage. In the midst of the pain, James managed to throw a blind punch and connected. The blow was followed by a grunt, and the sparks ceased.

James let out a grunt as he winced. He lifted a hand to his neck, still stunned by the pain. He tried to remember the last time he'd felt pain like that. There was a memory of a rope burn some odd five years ago. He was in the Clover Academy after his time in the army.

"You little bastard," he said under his breath, nursing the burn. "You have a frickin' chainsaw on your arm?" Not only that, that little bastard had tried to chainsaw his head off. "What the hell, man?"

He looked up only to find 0397 running to the other end of the parking garage. He looked back at James, a horrified look on his face. Had he never seen a Transhuman before?

"Stop playing around now." James stopped cold in his tracks when 0397 climbed to the edge of the garage's balcony. "Get down from there. We're fifteen stories up!"

0397 looked down and then back at James, weighing his options.

"Stop." James took a step closer and extended his hand to 0397. "Just let me help you."

In a single motion, the kid took a step back and fell off the building.

"No!" James rushed to the ledge, his heart at his throat, his voice filling the parking garage, loud and unrecognizable.

When he looked over the edge, he saw a spot of dirty blond hair down below. 0397 landed on the ground unharmed. He sprang back up and made a run for the dark alleys. Suspect 0397 disappeared out of James' line of sight as he reached for his radio.

Her laugh was almost a purr, smooth like blended Scotch. From the other side of her frequency, James' voice announced the target escaped him and made his way to the Development District. She had to laugh. Could this night get any worse?

Their response time had been damaged by their own division, their resources stretched, and now their Unit Leader had lost track of their high-priority target. Of course, it all had to happen on the most important mission the Deltas had ever seen. What else could she do but laugh? Writing the mission report and presenting it to the Military Department Directors would be even better. She felt sorry for the poor sucker that would have to write it because it sure as hell wouldn't be her.

Lying over the cold surface of a building's rooftop, Robin reached into her field weapon's case. Among all the jet black accessories, guns, and knives, her gaze glazed over the Scorpion's Tail. The rope dart came as a present after she graduated from the Academy. The characteristic prism tip was made of stainless steel to be light and precise. The silver rings and chain were reinforced to never come apart. The obsidian handle and the purple silk flag were luxuries, a personal gesture from her adoptive father.

Robin couldn't remember the last time she'd used the Scorpion's Tail. It was a complement to her abilities, and she was only supposed to use it when her commander approved or in life-or-death situations. She made a mental note to grab the rope dart in case of a confrontation. For now, she'd stick with looking for their target in the lowest area of the city, and she'd settle for firearms. She took a new rifle scope and installed it.

Robin searched through yellowing empty streets filled with trash and cracks on the pavement. The dark alleys showed her the sadness that was the Development District. In the distance, over the bridge and the polluted lake, City Hall shined like a beacon. Its lights beamed in the night sky, making the white stone gleam against the rich green of the surrounding parks. It felt so far away as if she were in a different but forgettable city. Robin searched her gut for a feeling, one of those sensations she'd heard heroes feel. Nothing.

That was okay. Her face twitched with indifference. They weren't there to save anyone, and she never felt much of anything anyway. Not really.

The radio frequency crackled in her ear. "Tiger to Komodo, do you copy?"

A smirk spread across her face, her eyes staying focused on the streets. "I copy. Go ahead, Tiger."

"What's your status?"

"Still no sign of 0397."

Robin could almost see his face, worried and furrowed. She pictured him frantically trying to figure out a strategy on the fly. She almost felt bad for him.

"Roger that, Komodo. I'll check with you again shortly. Tiger out."

The sound in her ear died, and she was alone again.

Robin had hoped the team would head in a new direction after Fox onboarded Alyssa into their Unit. One of the Deltas' biggest and most recent obstacles was that the company wouldn't send a team of two GENEs into field missions. Too many casualties had happened that way. And then Alyssa joined them, and they received the call for the Blue Flamingo case. She was sure then that the future for the Deltas was getting brighter. Robin aimed the rifle's scope to the far corners of the Development District. Some things never changed. Robin could have raised a glass to old times, to things staying the same, and drink to the oh so early death of her career.

Cheers, she thought while switching lenses. She was ready to give up on the streets that refused to give up any useful leads.

And then she saw it. Movement on Oak Street caught her attention. She zoomed in and saw a streak of yellow hair running to one of the boarded outbuildings.

A smirk turned the edges of her mouth. "Cheers indeed."

Suspect 0397 jumped and latched himself onto a fire escape, stuck thanks to years of built-up rust. He climbed to the top of the building and looked behind him. He examined the streets, checking to see if James had followed. No chance. He was too fast for poor James to catch up.

Me, on the other hand— Robin bolted the rifle. A clatter and a click guided her finger to the trigger.

Her target stood on that rooftop catching his breath, completely unsuspecting. She had a clear shot to the head. The whole thing was so perfect it hurt in her jaw. One bullet and she could wrap the whole thing up now, be home for breakfast. But she couldn't. They needed the subject alive, and the caliber she was packing would kill him, regardless of where she aimed. She'd have to catch him another way.

Suspect 0397 ran at full speed to the next building and leaped in the air, landing on the roof with a shoulder roll before running to jump to the next. He planned to make his escape through the rooftop jungle that was the Development District. Harder to get tracked that way, she supposed, if regular law enforcement were following. Robin smirked. He really didn't know who was after him.

She turned her radio on. "Silver Komodo reporting. I've got eyes on Target."

"HQ to Komodo. Triangulating your position now." Honey's voice in her ear went silent for a second. "All Delta units report to the Development District. Komodo, you have orders to intercept Target."

"Engaging in minus five minutes."

"Godspeed."

Robin pulled a rappel gun from her belt and shot at a neighboring building where she suspected her target would land next. If she had predicted his trajectory correctly, she should be able to intercept him there. She jumped and slid over the rappel cable, the night air biting at her face as she picked up speed.

When she was close to her destination, Robin fired a bola snare. The weapon flew out of her hand and wrapped around 0397's legs. His jump intercepted, he fell to the roof. Robin unfastened herself from the cable, coming down on the hard concrete with a delicate and quiet slap-out landing.

She turned to 0397 with a hand over the gun at her hip. He was still lying on the roof, his eyes full of confusion.

"Put your hands behind your back," Robin ordered, but she didn't move a step closer.

She pointed her gun at him and pulled out a pair of inhibitor cuffs. Their design suppressed whatever abilities a GENE had. Even if this guy was a new variation of GENE, his abilities had to have the same genetic source.

Comprehension ran across 0397's face. He understood the

gist of what she wanted, but not her words. James was right: this kid didn't have a translator. How primitive.

He looked up at her, eyes filled with an aggression worthy of a predator. There was something familiar about those steel-gray eyes. Something stirred at the back of her brain, her heart rate increasing. It was the same curiosity a snake felt when she found another in the wild. An instinct to dominate the other as the ultimate threat.

She laughed.

In a flash, 0397 rolled over onto his side and somehow cut himself free from the snare. She shot at him three times, but none of her bullets hit the target. Her opponent cut the distance between them before Robin could realize, and he disarmed her in two moves. He crunched the gun with his silver grip and slapped the inhibitor cuffs out of her hands.

Robin jumped back from 0397. She glanced around for the inhibitor cuffs. No luck. They were lost somewhere on that rooftop, cloaked by the dark of night. She'd have to find some other way to apprehend him.

"That was my only pair of cuffs, you brat." She scoffed and put her guard up, her right fist shielding her face. "Have it your way, then."

Robin jumped straight at the blond. She delivered all her martial art moves with deadly accuracy while she analyzed him. There was more to her opponent than his fancy arm. He too harnessed a powerful left kick. Robin guessed he hid more mechanical parts, and imagined a shiny leg under his dirty fatigues. The kid also had some level of military-grade training, but nothing too fancy. He was fighting on the defensive, nursing his left side. He was a fast fighter, but not operating at top speed. He was tired and wounded, his mind focused on getting away. Taking him down shouldn't be too hard.

Robin went in at full force, slithering past his defenses. She connected once on the lip, twice on the gut. When his defenses were down, she moved in with a roundhouse kick delivered to his hurt side. A dirty move, but it did the job of making 0397 cry out and fall to one knee, clasping his side.

"Had enough?" She approached him to finish the job. A good chop to the back of the head would knock him out cold. She could save the day, get the bad guy, and all that crap. Let the masses cheer.

0397 connected a punch with his metal arm to the pit of her stomach. Victory was so close that his retaliation brought a bitter taste to her mouth. The punch drove the air out of her. She retreated, fumbling for her gun while trying to refill her lungs.

Suspect 0397 stood up straight and, in one single fluid movement, threw something drenched in blue light at her. She rolled out of the way. Where did it come from? No chance to examine the weapon. It must have been one of the plasma disks James reported about over the radio.

Where the hell were her reinforcements? She looked up and saw her opponent panting, recovering faster than her. She decided then this was a life-or-death situation.

Robin forced herself to focus on the cyan shine coming at her. She lifted her unprotected hand in the air and caught the weapon in between her fingers. The light died in her hand. Warm liquid ran all the way down to her forearm. She stared at the dark purple venomous blood; its smell invaded her nostrils. Iron, primroses, and something like putrid flesh. Something woke inside her, dozing her with giddiness and an energy that wasn't there before. Her Artificial Euphoria activated from the depths of her modified genetic code. Robin squeezed the weapon, driving the sharp edges deeper into her hand.

0397 gaped at her, a priceless expression of confusion and fear.

"You wanted to play, Blondie?" A sizzling sound came from her wounds. "Welcome to the big leagues."

Robin threw the disk back at 0397, drenched in purple venom. Her opponent did well on his instinct and got out of the way. From his forearm, a blade came out, and it unfolded to create a sort of shield.

She raised an eyebrow at 0397's new line of defense. "I really didn't want this to get so messy, kid." She reached into her back pouch. "But you really leave me no choice."

In a fluid move, she let the Scorpion's Tail loose from its pouch, guided its prism tail up with a swing of its chain, and called it back home to her hand.

"Never seen one of these?" Robin asked when she saw the cautious curiosity on her target's face. "They're rare because they're flexible weapons. People think swords and knives are far more dangerous than a rope dart because they don't understand the danger of an unpredictable weapon. Especially when you add an extra punch." She drenched the tip of the dart in her blood and let the flag hang over it, hiding the danger away from prying eyes.

With a flick of her wrist, the poison dart hissed through the air towards the enemy. The purple flag fluttered behind it like wings. The poisoned prism clashed against the metal of 0397's shield. Robin flicked it back to her; she'd have to wait for an opening. She controlled the dart's trajectory by making circles in the air, a deadly gymnast's ribbon. She caught movement from the corner of her eye. 0397 fired four new plasma disks at her. She maneuvered the tail around and hit one of the weapons flying to her. She rolled out of the trajectory of the other three, never losing control of the Scorpion's Tail.

With 0397 focused on throwing another bout of disks at her, Robin switched to the offensive once more. She wrapped the chain around her neck to cut the tail's range. With a fluid yet precise move, she guided the point of the Scorpion's Tail. The dart passed over 0397's shield before he could raise it. He turned with the dart's trajectory, trying to move his face away, but the tip of the tail still bit him on the cheek. A thin scratch, but that was enough.

Robin called the Scorpion home. The fight was over.

Her vision blurred, and Robin realized the fight was not the only thing that came to an end. The adrenaline rush that gave her Enhanced performance and resistance was thinning, and she was crashing. It was the biggest downside to her abilities: she needed to finish the job before she fainted.

From one blink to the next, 0397 bent double in pain. He collapsed and screamed bloody murder. Robin knew a burning sensation invaded his face and was spreading all over his body. That was only the beginning.

She loomed over 0397. "I wish you wouldn't scream so loud; my head's pounding."

0397 screamed on, clawing at his face in agony.

Robin touched her head and winced. "Well, Blondie boy, if you hadn't thrown my cuffs away, we could have been done a lot faster." She crouched next to him and examined his symptoms. "Now we have to wait until you paralyze. If I give you the antidote now, you're sure to run away."

The place where the Scorpion's Tail had hit him left an ugly purple mark. The veins bulged around the wound as antibodies tried desperately to fight the unknown agent in the bloodstream.

"It must be a strange feeling," she almost whispered in fascination as he clawed at his face. "I wonder what it feels like to be poisoned. I have a high tolerance for most toxins myself, so I've never felt this."

A wave of exhaustion inundated her. She gave up on crouching and sat down on the cold rooftop.

"Can you hurry it up, kid? You're not the only one that

needs medical attention." She used the ledge of the building as a backrest.

Robin sent a silent alarm to the rest of her team, too tired to make a full report of her situation. This kid was taking an awfully long time to get to the paralyzing stage. Or was that time stretching because she felt so slow? The world around her grew woozy and strange. Perhaps she would close her eyes, just for a second. Maybe the world would stop spinning so much.

"Come in, Komodo. Come in."

The voice drifting in from far away was unrecognizable. She wasn't sure where she was or what was happening. The heat licking at her skin stirred up a memory of the depths of a jungle. There had been heat on her skin then, and sweat on her forehead dripping over her eyes. She'd thought a heat like that one was unnatural. The silence in the jungle was unnatural, too. Had the jungle been like that before the human race almost came to its extinction? No. The War had made it so, kept it wild but made it empty. They said the radiation from the ships had cleared out by the time she visited the place, an assault rifle in her hands and a full Omega Unit of twelve people behind her. James was there, too. Big and strong, but not as strong as he was now. She didn't have the poison inside her, either. They came out of that jungle together. The only ones standing. So much death around them, so much pain and blood.

"Komodo, come in. Are you injured?"

There was that voice again, so close to her ear. Her mouth was so dry, like she'd eaten wood shavings. She felt like there was something really important that she needed to be doing. Time swirled around her. Her mind drove in circles around mismatched memories and ideas. She landed again on James. She felt like he was supposed to be there, so she could tell him something important. What was taking him so long? If she could feel anything but drunken weakness, she'd resent him for not getting to her sooner.

"Robin?" His voice crackled in her ear. "Talk to me, Robin."

She came to with a gasp for air. Her heart jumped to her throat. All the knowledge of the last ten minutes of her life came rushing back. Robin opened her eyes. How long had she been out? She looked for 0397 next to her, where she'd left him, hoping he was still alive.

He was gone.

Her stomach dropped. Robin looked around the rooftop for him. She'd poisoned him. He was supposed to paralyze and die unless the antidote was administered. She fumbled for the vial at her hip, the one with the antidote for her venom. Still there, unused. What the hell was happening?

"Robin?!"

"I'm here..." she managed to say into the radio.

"Are you injured?"

"Yes..." She sighed, still weak.

"Where are you? The team tried to track you, but your GPS is nonresponsive."

Robin looked at her shoulder pad where one of 0397's disks had hit her. He'd hit the GPS chip on her shoulder pad and damaged it.

"James, he's gone. It's not working."

"What's not working?"

"The poison! You need to find him and give him the antidote."

"What? He can't be gone if you poisoned him. Where are you?"

"No, listen to me!" She hated the sound of her own voice then, tired, panting, slurred. "I poisoned him, and somehow, he's gone. I don't know how, but you need to find him."

"Don't worry about it. We'll find him, but you need to tell me where you are first."

Robin's vision unfocused again. She delivered static into the radio when she failed to speak.

"Stay with me, Robin."

"Elm Street and Barnes. Rooftop."

"I'm on my way. Stay with me, Robin."

Before the world became dark again and James' words drifted off, Robin hoped they'd find 0397 in time. Whatever was happening with that kid, the poison was still inside him. It would kill him eventually, and then writing that report would really be a mess.

CRIMSON_

Alyssa and her Omega units rushed back to the untagged Jeep as their mission switched gears once again. They blazed through downtown with the sirens on and picked up James on their way to the Development District. A whirlwind of emotions made Alyssa's head swirl as she tried to catch up. She knew missions under the Special Response Units were fast-paced and ever-changing. But this mission felt extreme. They had gone from tracking to a crisis in a matter of minutes. Was this really how it was supposed to be?

Commander Fox briefed them over the Jeep's intercoms. After several minutes of radio silence, Robin joined the call, confirming she was hurt and that their suspect was on the run again. Their orders were to get to the last place Robin checked in and split up.

"Tiger." Fox's voice reached them from the intercom. "We don't have time to call a Chemical GENE support squad. You're the only one in the team trained to deal with Komodo's poison, and your Transhuman traits protect you from the toxic gases in her blood. Grab an Omega and bring her back to HQ. We need to assess her status as soon as possible."

"Roger that, Commander," James answered from the back seat.

"Crimson."

Alyssa shifted on the passenger seat at the mention of her code name.

"You're our last line of defense and our most powerful weapon."

Alyssa's stomach went to knots. How did everything go so wrong? She was the last line between failure and success on her first field mission ever.

"There's a very slim chance 0397 is immune to the poison. It's far more likely he's got a high tolerance. We run the risk of him escaping or dying if we don't find him soon," he continued. "Use the toxicity radar to find him. When you do, we can't take any chances. Your orders are to engage on sight. I'm granting you GENE clearance."

The blood left her limbs. He was granting her permission to use her powers. Last time she used her abilities, people called her unreliable and volatile. Last time she used her abilities, she'd been transferred to the US branch, discarded by every other division like a piece of shiny trash.

"GENE clearance, sir?" She let the question slip out, hoping that perhaps she'd heard wrong.

There was a pause from the other side, and Alyssa hated how much she must've sounded like a child.

Fox's voice came back, firm but not unkind. "You've got Enhancements, right, soldier?"

"Yes, sir."

"Then use them. Shoot the target on sight."

The knot in her stomach tightened, and her face grew hot as she listened to the transmission die.

"Well, that's that," James spoke from the back. He consulted his GPS. "Omega Two, turn the sirens back on and keep driving south on this street. We can get to Robin's location faster if we take Jefferson."

"You got it," the Omega soldier said, and the blare of the emergency sirens boomed through the streets.

Alyssa checked out from the briefing James was giving that Omega soldier. She rode in silence, her mind still trying to wrap her head around the details of 0397's latest escape. This time, he was not only hurt but also poisoned. Somehow, he managed to get away from the two veterans in the Unit. Why would a confrontation with her be any different?

Our most powerful weapon. Fox's words echoed in her mind.

Try most unreliable, she thought. Inside of her lived a raw power she'd never managed to control. The consequences of losing control of her powers could be dire. She shook her head. Why was this happening? Robin should have been the one to catch their suspect. How had he been able to escape her too?

"I thought Robin's venom paralyzed the victim," she blurted out, not really meaning to say the words out loud.

"It does." James' voice reached her from the back seat.

"Then how is this happening? Can this guy really have a tolerance to it?"

"I don't know. I can't think of a single time the poison hasn't worked, but that doesn't matter now."

Alyssa looked at James through the side mirror. What mattered now was finding Robin and making sure she was fine; 0397 had become a secondary mission in his mind. Even if he couldn't say it out loud, Alyssa saw it all over his face.

"You're right." Alyssa nodded, committing to rolling with the punches. "We just need to focus on the mission for now. We'll find them." The last part of her statement felt more like a wish said out loud.

James gave her an almost apologetic smile. "You're our last line of defense, Crimson Thunder."

Alyssa chuckled. "Our most powerful weapon." The words tasted of vile at the back of her mouth.

Through the side mirror, Alyssa watched James jump down from the Jeep before it had fully stopped. His image distorted as he ran to the building on the corner of Elm Street, a yellow emergency bag at his shoulder.

As they sped away, she hoped James would reach Robin in time. She decided to trust that Robin would be fine. After all, Alyssa had her own mission to think of. She had the words "GENE clearance" to worry about.

Another wave of anxiety rushed through her as she pictured an encounter with 0397, one that would push her to use her abilities. The time to use her powers on a field mission had always been somewhere on the horizon. She just never expected it to come so soon, much less all at once.

Alyssa realized she just might start hyperventilating. *Get a hold of yourself,* she thought.

"We've reached the Industrial Sector, ma'am." The Omega soldier interrupted her anxious thoughts.

"Kill the lights, please." Alyssa tried to sound commanding, but giving orders still felt awkward in her mouth.

From the glove compartment, she pulled the toxicity radar and fired it up. The red screen on the front of the dusty, black box turned on with an infrared light. She set the reading's setting to toxicity levels. Robin's poison code was saved as a default setting. It was an archaic radar and barely a step up from heat radars, but it was still capable of showing the spectrometry of the landscape. Robin's poison would show based on the effects it had on the human body. The radar would look for feverish temperatures and toxic gases in the subject's blood.

As the untagged vehicle drove through the beaten-down streets, Alyssa realized why the Industrial Sector was referred to as New Graysons City's biggest failure. The sector sat at the edge of the Development District and once promised to house factories and new job opportunities. The buildings just stood there now, empty and decaying with humidity, a reminder of an unfulfilled promise.

"He shouldn't be hard to find. These streets are empty, and he seems to have a habit of making himself noticed." Alyssa wished she could stop sounding like she was willing things to happen.

They drove in darkness, the sparse streetlights guiding their path. The sky above them looked congested with olive-gray clouds. In the distance, thunder rumbled, announcing a late November storm. She watched the decaying streets, her eyes shifting between the darkness in front of her and the toxicity radar.

Beep.

The radar broke the silence and amped the tension in the Jeep.

"I've got something." Alyssa's voice was almost a whisper while she consulted the radar.

A red mark appeared on the screen. She watched it move in stunted strides. When she zoomed in on the picture, she saw a purple mark. Robin's venom running through his veins made it easier to spot him.

"Stop the car," she commanded as her eyes locked on the red and purple mark on her radar. "We've got him."

• • •

The alley was a labyrinth of brick walls and fire escapes. A public streetlight blinked from the other end, showering the alley with intermittent bouts of orange light. Alyssa approached the alley, a yellow emergency bag strapped to her back. Caution guided her every step as her eyes focused on the figure atop a fire escape.

Suspect 0397 stood in place with his back to her. He held onto the escape's metal rails as if to keep his balance. He took another step down the stairs and stopped, leaning against the rails to not fall. He was crashing under the venom's effects. Whatever tolerance he might have had was thinning. How long would he last without the antidote? Maybe her abilities wouldn't be necessary. The orange light at the end of the alley illuminated the whole corner again. It shined on his arm, a metallic glint proper of a gun.

You've got Enhancements, right, soldier? Fox's words came back at her, biting like the cold of the coming storm. Waiting out might still give him a chance to use his own abilities against her. And she had her orders.

Alyssa took off her gloves. The thumping of her heart gave way to a pit of emptiness in her stomach.

After the deepest breath she'd ever taken, she felt the energy surge through her body. Alyssa could hear herself breathe, and time around her slowed. A second life force awoke inside her. It ached in her stomach, in her teeth, and in her every limb. Dark red sparks came out of her fingers, electricity cracking and clacking. She made a claw with her hand as if holding a tennis ball. The bright red energy focused on the empty space in her hand.

Her eyes locked on the metallic orange flashes at the other end of the alley. Her presence hadn't gone unnoticed, not with the light show in her hand. 0397 turned to her, mesmerized as if he were trying to decide if what he was seeing was real or not. Alyssa held onto the electricity and aimed at the fire escape as she prepared to throw the concentrated mass of energy. The impact would throw 0397 down and stun him instead of killing him. Hopefully.

The electricity screeched as she let it loose. The metal rails crackled with the strenuous impact, echoing along the empty streets. Gray smoke and brick dust exploded from the alley's depths. Car alarms blared around them. The streetlight gave a final blink before dying out.

"Oh god," she gasped. Too much. She'd overdone it. She held onto the electricity for way too long and lost control. Just like last time. Tears welled up in her eyes. Was he dead?

Alyssa stayed glued to her spot, waiting for the cloud of debris to clear. Rain poured from the sky in heavy droplets, showering the scene clear of smoke. The energy inside her died out, like a well gone dry. The ache in her body grew; she could have dropped to her knees and cried in the rain. She bit her lip, forcing her feelings down, and waited.

Red sparks still sprung from the metal staircase, now burnt and barely hanging from the wall. The thought of protecting the GENE secrecy floated around her head. Who would cover up the electric explosion and her crude, red-bright lighting?

With shaking hands, she clicked the silent alarm button on her radio, signaling her Omega soldier to circle back around. She'd need help transporting 0397 to the Clover Building, in whatever state she'd found him. Alyssa turned on her shoulder flashlight and the one on her automatic before venturing deeper into the alley.

Bits of bricks littered the alley. The sparks of her electricity crackled around her as she passed by. Suspect 0397 was collapsed at the end of the alley. He'd jumped down the fire escape but was still hit by the explosion's shock wave. He managed to sit up while leaning against the wall. Alyssa shined her gun's flashlight over 0397. He covered his eyes with a bloody hand and winced, like the movement was too much to bear. Among the bruises and cuts, a purple mark stood out over his face. It had extended over his cheek and made its way to the nape of his neck. When his eyes adjusted to the flashlights, 0397 examined her with a distrusting look. Alyssa's heart drummed as she held the blond's gaze.

0397 coughed blood up along with a dry laugh. He rattled off a curse with his hoarse voice. "Now she wants to use the gun? Give me a break."

Alyssa recognized his words. She was rusty in German, but she spoke it well enough. She was the team's linguist, after all.

She signaled to his legs, blood and dirt staining his fatigues. "Can you move your legs?" Her best German came out rusty, her accent atrocious.

0397's eyes widened in surprise. His voice carried an unexpected tone of relief. "Are you German?"

Alyssa tried to imagine how it would feel to be chased, poisoned, and attacked with electricity, all in one night. She then thought about living through that without understanding a word of anything. The relief he must feel at finally understanding someone's words overwhelmed her.

"British, but I speak the language. Now, can you move?"

He winced after trying and shook his head. The poison had finally paralyzed his arms and legs.

Putting her gun away, she knelt next to him. "I'm here to help you." She ignored his unbelieving scoff and set the yellow emergency bag next to her.

She pulled the antidote from her bulletproof vest. When she reached to take his pulse, cold metal wrapped around her wrist. 0397 could still move his metal arm, but Alyssa suspected he wasn't as strong as usual.

Cold gray eyes locked on her blue with feral and untamed force. "What is that?"

"The cure. For the venom."

His eyes were steely cold, like the rain falling over them. Alyssa sensed a fearful disregard from him for the contents of her bag and for everything she represented.

"I'm really here to help you." She held his gaze. "Now you can let me, or you can die."

He eased his grip on her hand to let her work. When she touched him, she felt the cold water run in rivulets over his hot skin. He was running a high fever as his body tried to fight the toxins in his blood.

She could feel 0397's eyes examining her, trying to read her. "What happens now?"

Alyssa looked at him, weighing if she should answer. She'd almost fried the guy to death; answering his questions was a small kindness.

"I take you into headquarters."

"Are you the cops? The army?"

"Something like that." She ripped a gauze out of a sterilized package with her teeth. "I imagine they'd want to talk to you... about tonight."

"Tonight." He took her words in as if he was just realizing what he'd done. "And then what?"

Alyssa cleaned the side of his neck. "It is not for me to say." She took the syringe out of its casing.

A heavy silence fell upon them, the seriousness of the situation sinking in.

"I'm not going back," he said, his voice drenched in fever and fear. "I'm not done fighting."

"You are." Alyssa jammed the needle in the side of his neck. "At least for tonight."

Suspect 0397 was so far gone in his fever that he didn't even wince. Alyssa started to work on his other wounds. The one at his side was an especially nasty one. It looked deep and like he had burned it to try and cauterize it. She pulled a quick wound-sealing patch from her yellow bag. It would hold him until the doctors at the Clover building could patch him up. As she worked, she heard his breathing pattern regulate to long and peaceful breaths. His heart rate stabilized, the antidote lulling him into wellness.

"I think..." he said, his voice drunk with tiredness. "I made a mistake tonight. I lost control."

Alyssa stopped working and looked at him. She thought of the videos Fox showed them during the briefing. A cold and calculating weapon. Why was it that he looked so different now? He didn't look out of control in those videos, but she guessed control could mean different things for everyone. Control, to her, meant never using her abilities.

"There were plenty of mistakes made tonight."

The sound of the Clover emergency sirens drifted in. That would be her backup.

0397 smiled a tiny smile, his eyes watery and full of confusion. When he spoke, he did it without any harshness. "You have the bluest eyes I've ever seen."

Where Alyssa had once seen a feral killing machine, she now saw a regular guy. Just a kid with powers. Just like her.

MIGUEL_

A fluorescent bulb buzzed as it showered the tiny bathroom's tile walls with depressing gray light.

Just dreams, Miguel thought while looking at his reflection in the mirror over the sink, disconcerted.

A bruise on his side marked the place where Shadow Braid checked for broken ribs in his dreams. For two weeks, Miguel had dreamed the same dream. Every night, he found himself on that same strange beach and followed Shadow Braid away from the tropical storm. Every night, the hole in the sand opened, and she extended her hand, inviting him to follow. Every night, he refused her. He'd wake up with a gasp, sweating and tangled in bedsheets. He always ran to the bathroom and splashed cold water over his face, trying to calm his racing heart.

It was just a dream, Miguel tried to convince himself as he examined the bruise on his side, his heart still racing in his chest.

The red and purple mark extended over his ribs, broken blood vessels spotting the area. His injury first appeared like a shadow, dark but soft, after the first dream. It looked like a suggestion of where the real bruise would appear. With every passing day, the mark only got worse.

Maybe he'd hit himself while doing drills—the Academy had started to give him military training, and those drills were brutal. Of course, he didn't remember hitting his side that bad. What if he'd gotten it after a radiation session? It could be a side effect of the radiation bombarding his body. This hadn't happened before, though. Come to think of it, he didn't bruise often. He slid his fingers over his skin and felt a pang of pain.

Miguel exchanged a worried look with his own reflection. Brown eyes stared back at him, red specks dotting the inner circle of his iris. Maybe his dreams were not dreams after all.

He covered his bruise with his shirt and turned away from his reflection. There had to be a better explanation for what was happening to him. It was dumb to think Shadow Braid was real. It was stupid to consider the beach with dying jellyfish existed. It was kid stuff.

Resolving to go back to bed, Miguel turned off the bathroom light. His naked feet guided him across the cold wood-look floor. City light gleamed through the window walls of his Clover-issued studio apartment. He stopped in front of his bed to look at the storm looming over the city. Lighting cracked somewhere in the distance, like an open vein across the sky.

Enhancements sometimes affected people's minds. Was he going crazy? Recurrent nightmares were one of the symptoms Doctor Sharp always checked for. To entertain the idea of Shadow Braid being real had to be a sign of insanity.

An otherworldly weight on his shoulders dragged him down as he sat on the bed. Unanswered questions ran through his head like wild coyotes chasing prey. What if his Enhancements were melting his brain? What then?

Frustration grew in his chest. If only there were an easier way to answer all of his questions by himself. He pressed his eyes with the heels of his hands. What would happen to him if he told the doctors about his dreams? Would they take him off the GENE program? His heart raced back up again. Cold sweat ran down his back. If he didn't get superpowers, he could never go back to San Gerónimo. He'd never find his family or fight for his people. He'd never be a hero.

As nausea welled up in his stomach, Miguel reached for the electronic tablet on his nightstand. He turned it on and landed back onto the comic book he had been reading before bed.

The colorful panels and his favorite heroes' feats to vanquish evil silenced the unanswered questions in his mind. Miguel smiled to himself as he reread the latest chapter of *Rangers of Earth*, Issue No. 134. During an epic battle with the monster Zetslen, Terra's friends came back just as everything seemed lost. They came back for Terra, and the day was saved. Relief washed over him like a drink of water on a hot day.

With his heart rate back to normal, he stopped reading. An idea stirred in the back of his mind. There might be a way for him to find out the answers to all the questions he had. He clicked on his tablet a couple of times and opened an email he'd received about a month ago.

Hi Miguel,

I was thrilled to hear you loved Rangers of Earth! I had a feeling you would. I'm attaching the rest of my electronic issues for you to read; please think nothing of it. I also wanted to pass along the department's virtual scheduler. Here, you'll be able to request appointments outside of our regular schedule. Please do not hesitate to come to me with any emergencies or questions.

Bon appétit!

Doctor J

Johannes Kingstone

Head of Genetic Research and Laboratory, Clover Co. Medical Department

Miguel considered the doctor's email. He liked Doctor J. He wasn't like the other adults in the medical staff who were only concerned with his Enhancements. He just might be cool enough to answer his questions without interrogating him in return. Miguel clicked on the link and scheduled an appointment. He turned the tablet off and went to bed, hoping for a dreamless sleep. He drifted off easier than he had on previous nights.

A sweet orange smell hung in the air with underlying tones of antibacterial soap and rubbing alcohol. As he sat on the cold metal examination table, soulful lyric-less music played in the background. It made Miguel think of a beach party under an orange sky, the last rays of sun gleaming on moist sand. He pictured people in purple sunglasses swaying to the rhythm of brass guitars while drinking green tea lattes from golden chalices, like a modern version of the parties in Greek myths.

The bright light from the doctor's penlight passed over his eyes once more.

"Ah! There it is," Doctor Johannes Kingstone said triumphantly, a slight Caribbean accent in his voice. "Your iris is changing color."

The doctor finished checking Miguel's eyes and walked to his desk. "The effects of the dilation will wear off in about twenty minutes." Doctor Kingstone reached for his electronic tablet to take notes. "Until then, your vision might be a little fuzzy."

He turned the volume down on the speaker behind him and Miguel wished he hadn't. Doctor J's music always improved his visits. The doctor finished with his notes and came around the desk. He faced Miguel and sat on the edge of the desk, placing his stylus behind his ear.

"So, tell me. What brought you to my office today? We weren't due for a visit until next week."

Miguel's mouth grew dry. "Well, I noticed my eyes were getting red, and I wasn't sure if that was supposed to happen." He shrugged. "You said I could come if I had questions."

The doctor offered him a warm smile. "I'm glad you came then. It's very important that we monitor your progress. You will see some changes in your body, and I don't want you to have any concerns."

Miguel smiled back, hoping it looked genuine.

"The change of color in the eyes is the first sign that the Enhancement Process is progressing as expected." The doctor continued, "To see unnatural colors present in the iris is a common side effect of the Enhancements. It depends on the genetic modifier we're harvesting."

"Is red common?"

"Hmm, not really. Common colors are gold, purple, and electric blue. Red is part of a new variation we're trying."

Miguel nodded, pretending to absorb the details the doctor had given him so far. If he had gone there to only talk about the changing color of his eyes, this new information would be exciting. He'd want to know more about what kind of powers he might get. But he was there to find out something else.

"So, do all GENEs go through the same thing?"

"That's right. As you know, there are three known GENE classes: Transhumans, Chemicals, and Electrochemicals..." From his desk's drawers, the doctor pulled out a document and offered it to him.

The document was a colorful mind map titled "GENE Program Enhancement Timeline." Miguel had seen the diagram a couple of times before, but not in such a detailed format. The map divided the Enhancement Process into five stages: Prescreening, radiation, and the three different stages of mutation.

"The base for all GENE classes is the same, so the mutation process looks the same across the board," Doctor J said, his voice confident. "In your case, we are just at the end of the Radiation Stage. The change of color in your iris only means you're close to entering the First Mutation Stage."

Miguel gulped—he didn't realize they were this close to his first mutation. He should feel excited, but he felt a worry bubble in his stomach. "Will it hurt?"

Doctor Johannes took a moment to answer and gave him a relaxed smile. "I'll be honest with you. We can't know for sure. Sometimes, mutations can be painful, but some others manifest as a common cold would. Your GENE class is unpaved territory. We know it'll be a variation of an Electrochemical Enhancement, but we don't know how similar the process will be or what kind of abilities it will harvest."

Miguel's brow wrinkled as he contemplated the answer.

"I'll tell you what," the doctor continued with the same reassuring tone. "We'll monitor your mutation path. If your mutations begin giving you painful symptoms, we'll draft a plan for your recovery. I'll personally lead your recovery treatment, so we will see each other every day."

"Really?" A small smile appeared on Miguel's face.

"Of course! I'll bring my whole comic book collection—we'll have a blast."

"Okay." Miguel realized they'd gotten off track. How could he learn what he really wanted to know without revealing exactly what was going on? "What else can happen in the first mutation?"

"Well, there are different scenarios. I could give you the full list of side effects." He raised both eyebrows at Miguel. "Or you could tell me which particular side effect you're worried about."

Miguel bit his lower lip. Was he being too obvious? He chose his words carefully. "Mental issues."

"I see." Silence danced between them for an instant. "What kind of mental issues?"

"Doctor Sharp always asks about nightmares or hallucinations." He shrugged. "Is that part of the mutations?"

The doctor paused as if he were looking through his archives for a correct answer. "We've had cases of Transhumans reporting a sense of mania during their mutations. An on-top-of-the-world sensation that affects their decision-making and their ability to distinguish reality. What you're referring to isn't really part of the Enhancements, but a malfunction in the brain due to mutations. An unfortunate one, I'm afraid."

"So..." Miguel stretched his hands together. "What would happen if someone gets that side effect?"

"It varies from case to case." Doctor J cocked his head, narrowing his eyes.

Miguel held his gaze as neutral as he was able. He hoped the sweat on his forehead and the thumping of his heart weren't noticeable.

"Usually, we need to stop the Enhancement Process and assess the damage to a person's mind." The doctor continued, suspicion still latent on his face. "Some people don't make it back, especially when they go rogue and become violent, you know?"

Miguel did. He read between the lines and saw what Doctor Johannes wasn't saying. He figured there must be psychiatric evaluations, drugs, and studies. If that didn't work, there was one last thing Clover would do.

"The Exit Clause," Miguel said out loud, still looking the doctor in the eye.

Johannes Kingstone bit his lower lip for an instant as if he were trying to not say more and failing in the end. "That's right. The Exit Clause is the company's last resource when the subject becomes a danger to themselves, the public, and the GENE secrecy."

Miguel shuddered. Before he signed his contract with Clover, lawyers and other people in suits mentioned the Exit Clause. But they didn't tell him very much. He wasn't sure what it meant. He pictured someone pushing him outside the front door and locking it behind him, leaving him out on the streets, or perhaps deporting him back to Chile.

"I wouldn't worry too much about it, Miguel." The doctor interrupted his wild thoughts. "Mental malfunctions rarely happen at the high peak of the First Mutation Stage, but we have ruled out any high risks during the Pre-screening process and the Radiation Stage. Besides, the medical trials for your GENE class have all been successful. The risk of mental side effects are very low."

"But it could still happen." Miguel tasted the bile in the back of his mouth.

"It could. The likeliness of it is one in hundreds, though." The doctor searched his face. "I understand the whole thing about the Exit Clause sounds scary, so I get why you worry. Please know there are a lot of solutions we would try before going there, hundreds of them." He sighed. "On the off chance your Enhancements turned into a danger, Doctor Sharp and I would protect you. You have my word."

Miguel looked down at his red sneakers. He wanted to believe Doctor J. He could tell his favorite doctor all about the nightmares, his bruise, and his doubts about what was real and what wasn't. He knew Doctor J could make him feel protected, safe. But doubt still lurked in the back of his mind. What if Shadow Braid was real after all? Wouldn't it be better to find out on his own before asking the doctors for help?

A resolution settled in the pit of his stomach. That night, when Shadow Braid visited him in his dreams, he'd do what she asked. He'd follow her to find out whether she was real or not. If she wasn't, he'd return to Doctor J. and tell him everything.

Miguel looked up and returned the smile. "Thank you, doctor. I had been thinking about those side effects for a while, since I get asked every week and all. It really helped to talk to you."

The doctor tittered, pleased. "I'm glad to be of help."

Miguel jumped down from the metal table. "Yeah. Well, I guess I'll see you next week."

"You got it, pal." Doctor Kingstone stood up and went back to his seat behind the desk as Miguel made his way to the door. "Miguel?" he called one last time.

Miguel turned around, putting his most innocent blank expression on his face, "Yes?"

"There's nothing else you would like to tell me, right?"

Miguel stood there, reconsidering his choice again.

He gave the doctor a shy smile. "I was actually hoping to borrow more comic books from you. I finished the last issue you lent me last night."

T he interrogation room at the Clover Holding Facility contained only a table, a couple of chairs, and security cameras on every corner.

On the far left, two entrances stood out. A heavy black door opened for the interviewers. A white barred door led the way to a short row of holding cells. The lime light and the green of the walls made the room feel submerged in murky waters.

The room gave Alyssa the feeling of being inside an aquarium tank. They both served a similar purpose. A tank kept dangerous sea creatures under the pretense of conservation, but it was all for human amusement. The cells connected to the room and the detention center in Clover's basement kept rogue GENEs away from the public. The Military divisions liked to pretend this was for civilian safety, but it was all to protect the GENE secrecy.

After the apprehension of the suspect, Alyssa and her Omega backup rushed to the Clover Building. Even with the antidote running through his bloodstream, 0397 needed urgent medical attention. Health staff were already waiting for them outside of Clover's Medical Wing. Alyssa's heart hammered in her ribs as they rushed 0397 to the building's own ER. Before she could call it a night, Alyssa received another set of orders. Over the Jeep's intercom, Commander Fox tasked her with processing 0397 for an interview. He would conduct the interview himself.

Alyssa worked on a laptop set at the metal table in the middle of the interrogation room. If she had learned anything during her time in the Records Room, it was how to process an Enhanced suspect for an official interview. In only one hour, she requested the interrogation room, prepped the evidence for the interview, and filled the forms to get an old translator device. It would be a dusty old headset, but at least Fox would be able to use it to speak to 0397.

"Oh, bloody hell..." Alyssa whispered to herself as her laptop gave her an error message. The sync of the cameras to the Delta Unit server had failed again. The cameras and microphones in the interrogation needed to be ready to record the interview with 0397, but they weren't working for Alyssa.

With a few clicks on the laptop, she attempted to sync the recording equipment again. While the computer loaded, Alyssa massaged her forehead. The beginnings of a massive migraine had settled there. According to the laptop's side menu, it was 4:43 am. She had last slept a good three hours ago, but her tiredness and pain weren't coming just from her broken sleep schedule. Her body resented the raw electrical life force exploding from the depths of her genetic code.

Heavy with tiredness, her thoughts swam to the events of that night. She thought of 0397's words. *I made a mistake tonight. I lost control.* Alyssa wasn't sure she believed him, but she knew a thing or two about losing control. Hell, losing control of her abilities was what got her transferred to the other side of the Atlantic.

Regret swarmed inside her. She flexed the fingers of the

hand that had held the electricity that night. The lines on her palm ran deep, like carvings over sepia-brown driftwood. How did she lose control so fast? One second, she was holding onto a stable electrical current. The next, her energy left her hand and caused an electrochemical explosion.

An explosion like that one wasn't an easy thing to cover up, but Clover had the means to do it. As soon as Alyssa had confirmed their suspect had been apprehended, she heard over her radio that the Legal Department had deployed a cleanup crew. Despite being part of a separate department, these crews worked with the Military Department to hide any evidence of a GENE interaction with the general public. Alyssa was sure she'd eventually hear how the cleanup crew had a hard time cleaning up her little incident.

With a sigh of resignation, Alyssa pushed those thoughts away. She'd rather forget that she had used her abilities again. She'd rather forget that she had failed to control them again. At least for tonight.

Alyssa looked over the evidence she'd prepped for Fox, trying to keep her mind occupied. She had gathered snapshots from security videos, printed out a timeline of the incident, and straightened out other paperwork.

Blue Flamingo Incident, Alyssa read on the initial transcript of the mission's briefing. *An open attack on the nightclub's patrons reportedly led to a confrontation with New Graysons PD. No firearms or military-grade weapons were confirmed. Multiple reports confirmed injuries similar to stab wounds and burns.*

As her face twisted in a frown, Alyssa tried to imagine what had happened inside the Blue Flamingo Club. So far, the attack had been nondescript. Ambulances and paramedics had been called to treat over a dozen injured patrons. A police officer had been taken to a local hospital's ICU. But the source of their injuries was still unknown. She continued to read the transcript's printout.

Suspect 0397. John Doe. Young male, 5' 10", Genetically Enhanced Entity (GENE) confirmed. Missing translator device. Negative ID.

How odd was it really to find someone without a translator device on them? Especially someone that was Enhanced. Her investigative sense woke up. She'd think that whoever was behind 0397's Enhancements would have wanted to keep tabs on him. A translator chip would be the easiest way to track him.

Alyssa absently touched her own translator. The ear cuff mounted on her earlobe felt cold to the touch. She tried to remember when she'd gotten it and concluded it had been with her since birth. Did 0397 ever have one? Or did he rip his off? Fighting back a yawn, she told herself she'd find out those answers after Commander Fox spoke to 0397.

Her computer chirped, letting her know that the sync had been successful. Her job was done. Alyssa smiled, pleased to have technology finally work for her. Her tired body wanted nothing more than to head back to her apartment and get some rest, but her mind wanted answers. If she waited for Fox, perhaps he'd let her watch the interview.

The white barred door rattled open, making Alyssa jump out her stupor and her chair. Two Omega soldiers entered the room in their black uniforms. They carried a man between them, his head covered with a black hood. Alyssa's focus split between the flutter in her stomach and the hooded prisoner. She couldn't see his face, but she could still visualize the marks from their encounter earlier. A broken lip, bloody nose, and red brick dust in his hair.

"Ma'am." One of the soldiers saluted her; the red Clover logo embroidered over her chest caught the green light.

Alyssa saluted her back.

"The suspect's still under. The doctors assured us he wouldn't wake up for ten to twenty minutes. Where do you want him?"

It took her a second to process the question. They had brought him in sooner than she expected. "Over here, please." She motioned to the chair opposite hers.

They dragged him in, like dead weight, inhibitor cuffs at his wrists and feet. An unconscious 0397 was deposited on the chair in front of her. Alyssa watched as they bound him to the table. After seeing him survive Robin's poison, she doubted anesthetics would be effective for long. With another salute, the Omega soldiers exited the interrogation room through a heavy black door. A metallic echo declared the emptiness between the green walls.

Suspect 0397 leaned back in his chair, almost motionless, like a wax model. His chest moved up and down with the steadiness of his calm breathing. He'd been given new clothes. The blood-stained fatigues and gray shirt were replaced by a battleship-blue jumpsuit. The white lettering on the back read Clover Co. Holding Facility. Alyssa stole a glance at 0397's right arm. The alloy covering his arm extended past his sleeve, and it was unclear where the machine ended and the human began. Under the lime light, the arm looked almost liquid. Its unnatural shine sparked Alyssa's thoughts. 0397 had upgrades in his genetics, but most of them involved the use of the machine.

The black hood has to go, she thought as she stepped away from the interview materials. Fox would want to walk in, install the translator headset, and start talking to the subject right away. Alyssa let go of the air she was holding in her chest, slow and steady. She took a step closer to 0397 and reached for the hood. The fabric between her fingers was dark as velvet and rough as rope.

The light shone over 0397's eyes when she pulled the hood

off. He squeezed his eyes and moved a hand to try to protect his face from the light, finding it bound. Alyssa took a small step back and clutched the hood against her chest. 0397's eyes adjusted to the light and then locked on her. His gray eyes had that feral aggression she'd seen earlier in the briefing videos.

"Where...?" 0397 uttered the beginnings of a question in a raspy German. He looked her up and down, studying her, and croaked a different question. "Who are you?"

Alyssa's mouth went dry. She searched his face. No spark of recognition ever reached his eyes. Something was wrong.

Questions hung from the tips of her lips. She had to get out of there. Fox was the only one who could talk to the suspect now. If she stayed a minute longer, she might not be able to contain herself. With the black hood still in her hands, Alyssa turned away from 0397 and headed for the door.

The black door gave a loud bang behind her. Alyssa barely noticed she was stepping into the hall. She walked to the other end of the hall until she found the two-way mirror that served as a window to the interrogation room. The two-way mirror displayed a black screen on her side and a fake wall on the other. The room would continue to be invisible until Fox came in and flipped the switch on the other side.

She caught a glimpse of her reflection over the dark surface of the two-way mirror. All she could see were reflections of her own shape. The features made a suggestion of blurred lines by the orange light that glowed over her head. Even in the dimness, her red hair stood out like a thunderbolt in a dark and misty sky —a mark of sudden violence, cracking the skies open, wild and obscene.

Her mind swam with questions. Did 0397 really not know who she was?

The sound of precise steps against the concrete floor called her attention. Commander Fox approached her from the other end of the hall.

"Sir." Alyssa saluted him, and the flutter in her stomach came back. She hadn't seen the commander face-to-face since her little screwup with her powers. What was he going to do? Suspend her? Banish her back to the Records Room for another three months? She supposed that wouldn't be so bad. She'd be able to keep looking at her Enhanced Narcotics cases, just like before.

"What's the status of our suspect?" Fox still looked alert, even this late in the night. He carried a black case and a folder with paperwork under his arm. The case likely contained the old translator device she had requested for him.

"The cameras are synced and ready to record. The evidence you wanted is on the table. He's ready for you, sir."

"Excellent. Now go home and get some rest. I'll need you to write the mission report." He handed her the papers he carried under his arm. "Present yourself at the Delta Tactical Room tomorrow morning. I've arranged for you to be transferred from Records, permanently."

Alyssa took the papers and couldn't hide her confusion. Writing the mission report was a huge responsibility. It meant she'd be compiling evidence and suspect statements, and then presenting the case to the Department Directors. Fox was upgrading her to a full-fledged member of the Delta Unit. "Me, sir?"

"Yes. I want you to do more than just read old cases. Besides, it's only natural that you'd be the one to write the report since you brought the suspect in. Not bad for your first case."

Alyssa blinked twice. Not bad? Was he kidding? The only reason she'd brought 0397 in was because James and Robin had already slowed him down. Not to mention her electrochemical explosion. She'd probably fried the Industrial Sector power modules. He'd granted her GENE clearance, and she had failed at keeping her powers in check.

"Don't look so surprised, Crimson."

"My apologies, Commander." Alyssa tried to straighten her face, but her shock was hard to hide. "I just thought you'd have some feedback for me about the use of my powers. Given my history..."

She saw everything again in a millisecond. Her commanding officer yelling at her just inches away from her face in the training area. Nostrils flaring, spit splashing her cheeks. The anger growing inside her and the pain in her limbs. Red lightning exploding out of her. The smell of burnt hair and skin filling her.

"You mean that accident in the UK branch?"

Accident. She'd never heard it described with that word. Catastrophe, calamity. Those were the kinds of words she'd heard before.

The inside of her mouth grew thick, like she was eating molasses. "I shot at my commander officer. She was lucky I didn't kill her."

The commander held her gaze in silence. When he spoke again, his tone came out soft and reassuring. "Yes, and it was an accident. You are very powerful, Alyssa. No one should expect you will know how to harness that power right away, not even you."

His words chipped away at that block of guilt and shame she carried with her.

Commander Fox straightened up, the golden glint in his eyes still soft. "And as far as mistakes on the field, they happen all the time. We'll never get better by trying to avoid them." The Commander offered her a kind smile. "Perfection doesn't exist."

Alyssa returned his smile. "Thank you, sir." She looked down at the folder in her hands. The fluttering in her stomach came back with euphoric emphasis. He wasn't upset about her use of her powers, and now she had a chance to use her investigative background to do her job. This was it—the chance she'd wanted to start her new career in her own terms. "I can get on it right away. Maybe I can start by watching the interview?"

Fox chuckled and shook his head. "I appreciate the enthusiasm, but it's been a long night. Use the recording of the interview to write your report. But not until tomorrow." He lifted his eyebrows for emphasis on that last part. "Go home, soldier. That's an order."

"Yes, sir."

Alyssa watched him walk away. He entered the interrogation room through the black door. Questions still churned somewhere in her mind, but they would have to wait. She had her orders.

The room looked just like his: the lights of the city shone through the window walls, showering his studio apartment with white-orange gleams. His tablet and the dirty cereal bowl lay undisturbed on his modest nightstand. Just as he'd left them before falling asleep.

The place he woke in was an accurate copy of his living quarters, except for the creeping cold and the green spores raining down from the ceiling like flaky snow. There was also that doll at the foot of his bed.

The toy was the perfect size to fit into a child's hand. To Miguel, it looked like a Chinese princess. Its red tunic with golden dragons matched the roses on its head. Its long hair like silk draped over its tiny shoulder in an intricate design. In the shadows of his bedroom, all he could see of its face was the vivid red lips of a brush-painted smile.

When Miguel decided he'd follow Shadow Braid into the portal, he expected to see her right away. Instead, he slept a dreamless sleep for three nights in a row before Shadow Braid attempted contact again. And now, this doll appeared.

Curious, Miguel reached for the doll. A choking sound from

a dark corner stopped him. He looked up and found Shadow Braid staring him down. She wore a scowl on her face and the same hospital gown as before.

Miguel drew his hand back from the doll. "Sorry."

Shadow Braid came closer to the light, her moves stunted and mechanical. She cocked her head, still staring at him with cold, dead eyes. Her hair floated around her with a life of its own.

Miguel jumped out of bed. Why did he ever think this would be a good idea? "I'm ready to go with you." He gulped.

Something like a smile spread across Shadow Braid's face. She nodded and took a step closer towards him. Miguel felt a strange weakness in his chest. He looked back at his bed and saw a sleeping version of himself, just like he had when he first met Shadow Braid on that strange beach.

Shadow Braid lifted her palm in front of her and stared deep into Miguel's eyes. A breeze flew inside his living quarters, and time around them slowed. Something stirred within Miguel. An outside force drove his own hand up and pressed it against hers. Her cold skin brought back the memory of the stones at the edge of the Rio Grande. Miguel closed his eyes.

The sound of water running downstream flooded his senses. Miguel saw himself relive that day as if the memories belonged to someone else. The air smelled of damp earth, a cold September storm approaching from the edge of the border. The long caravan walked the stretch of the river. Miguel shivered in the dark of night; murky waters covered him up to his waist. He held his father's hand.

Like a river going back to sea, Miguel found his way back to Shadow Braid and the present. He felt linked to her as if he were sharing a part of his psyche with her.

Seagulls cried somewhere in the distance. Sea breeze carried a salty aroma around him. Miguel opened his eyes to find himself on an island. It was so bright that his eyes welled up as the humid air stuck to his skin. When his eyes adjusted, he could see a thin ribbon of rich blue waters merging with the sky on the horizon. They were deep into an island's wilderness, far from the coast.

Miguel looked down at his feet, the olive-brown of his skin contrasting with the fine white sand. He found two sets of footprints in front of him, marking a path to follow. The first set suggested a big and heavy body, perhaps a man's. The second was the smallest footprints Miguel had ever seen. A child's. He pictured a father and child walking hand in hand through the island, and his heart ached.

Shadow Braid hovered close to the smallest set of footprints. "These yours?" he asked.

She didn't look at him. She stared at the marks in the sand as if she could see her past self in them.

"Are you okay?" Miguel almost crouched, trying to meet her ghostly eyes.

Shadow Braid seemed to wake up from her trance when he spoke. She floated away from him, following the prints' path.

"I wish you could tell me where we're going!" he called after her, jogging to not be left behind.

The footprints led Miguel to the other side of a steep hill. He panted as he climbed. He cleaned the sweat off of his forehead with the back of his hand. His side burned from trying to catch up. He looked around for Shadow Braid.

His eyes followed the trail of prints in the sand and found first the Chinese porcelain doll laying on the hot sand, abandoned like it was disposable. Now it was wearing a white dress printed with blue and gold cranes, the colors as rich as the hues of the sky above. Miguel inspected the toy further. It was unharmed except for the fine sand speckling its abundant dark hair. Miguel had the instinct of picking it up, but something caught his eye beyond the doll and the hill.

It was a conglomerate of gray-and-white arched steel structures. The military compound looked like something pulled out from the memories of his life in San Gerónimo. Miguel stopped jogging, and then he saw Shadow Braid—she was floating towards the compound.

The armored cars, electric fence, and the watchtowers brought it all back. Labored breathing raised his chest. He commanded his feet to move with no luck. He heard his father's voice telling him to stay away from the green tents and to never look the Russian militia soldiers in the eye. Cold sweat trickled down his back. Images of mismatched riots and the sound of gunshots flooded his mind. There was also fire in his head; the image of red-orange, all-consuming flames churned behind his closed eyelids.

He told himself this wasn't the same compound of his past. This compound was on an island. Was it even real, or just part of this dreamlike world?

The answer to his own question hit him suddenly as if someone had just downloaded information into his brain. The compound was real. Just like his apartment, the places he visited with Shadow Braid were real. However, they weren't real *here*. Here, they were mere shadows of their real versions.

This was a shadow world.

The touch of a cool hand on his shoulder jolted him back to the present, wherever that was. When he lifted his eyes, he found Shadow Braid staring at him. Her eyes searched him, drilled into him as if trying to figure out what was wrong. The urge to run away intensified. It crawled through every inch of his skin, telling him he needed to leave. He needed to be away from this weird reality and from the memories of the Russian compounds in San Gerónimo.

But where would I run to?

He looked at the sands surrounding them. The baked-by-the-sun talcum powder extended for miles. There was nowhere to go but the compound, and he didn't know the way out of the shadow world. Miguel sighed the fear away.

"I'm fine," he said as he straightened his back. "Let's go."

Decontaminating mist showered them as they entered the compound. Miguel had expected to see soldiers running around cheap-looking stations, white sand lifting with their every move. But the place was still and empty.

The inside of the compound reminded him more of an empty hospital, of Clover's labs. It had the same white pristine tiles, the high-tech look, and the sterilized smell hanging in the air. The entrance to the compound looked just like the decontaminating area outside of the Radiation Room. The two places could have been exact standardized copies of each other.

Shadow Braid floated past him. Miguel had the impulse to stop her as if someone could catch them. He reminded himself they were in the shadow version of the compound. He followed her through the halls, the white tile cool against his naked feet.

They stopped in front of a door at the end of a hall. With a piece of gray tape and crude lettering, someone had labeled the room G.E.N.E.

The scent of rubbing alcohol slapped him in the face upon entering the G.E.N.E. room. Miguel half-noticed the mountains of puzzle games and the blackboards filled with words written in what he thought was Chinese. A heavy metal door rested on the far left, looking out of place as if it had been forced into that room. Shadow Braid stopped in front of that door and turned to him.

"Clover's Holding Facility..." Miguel read out loud from the copper plaque mounted on the door. "I don't understand. How did we get back to Clover?"

Shadow Braid pointed a delicate finger at his hand, and Miguel suddenly felt the sensation of holding something. It was his Clover ID badge.

He gasped out a giggle as if Shadow Braid had just shown him a card trick he couldn't figure out. "How'd you do that?"

Shadow Braid only pointed to the card reader attached to the door.

Miguel felt the same sense of information being downloaded into his brain as before. Shadow Braid hadn't said a word, but he understood what she was thinking. "You can't go in there without me."

Shadow Braid nodded. Miguel pieced something else together: She hadn't waited to take him to the shadow world because she needed his permission. She needed him to grant her access to whatever was behind that door.

Shadow Braid had had access to every other place. What was different about this one? And how was he supposed to help? Miguel had never been in the Clover's Holding Facility. He didn't know what was back there.

He tried to find the answer by calling the information to his mind like the other times. But it didn't come. If he wanted to find out what was behind that door, he'd have to follow Shadow Braid thoughtlessly again.

Miguel held his breath and passed his ID over the reader. The door opened with a sigh.

"Let's go over it one more time."

Commander Fox stood up from his seat at the metal table. His peaked cap sat at one end of the table, and evidence materials littered the metal surface in front of him. James watched through the two-way mirror.

Fox grabbed a photo from a manilla folder and placed it in front of 0397. "Is this you in the picture?"

Suspect 0397 looked up at Fox and not at the picture, tiredness evident in his hollow face. When he spoke, James heard German speech in one ear. There was a short delay while his translator picked up the signal of 0397's microphone. The words transformed into English for him to understand. It was like watching a cop movie with bad dubbing. "You've already asked this."

Fox ignored the comment. "Is this you in the picture?"

0397 slumped down until his forehead touched the table, his hands cuffed together with inhibitor cuffs. He gave a heavy sigh that needed no translation. "He looks like me, so I suppose it is me."

"These were taken from security footage that places you at

the Blue Flamingo." Fox placed a couple of other photos on the table. "So you had to be at the scene, correct?"

"I guess."

"What were you doing there?"

"I don't know." 0397 slowly sat back up.

"Why were you in the Arts District?"

"I don't know."

Fox let out a well-appointed scoff. "You don't seem to know very much. One might think you're hiding something, 0397."

The blond lifted his eyes from the pictures, his expression hard. "Don't call me that..."

"I'd call you your name if you knew it."

0397 looked down at his lap.

The commander walked around the table, his shoes clacking against the concrete floor like an impatient old-fashioned wristwatch. "Now..." Fox leaned in from behind the suspect and pointed at the pictures laid over the table. "You're in all these pictures and security videos, looking like a man on a mission. We know someone put you up to this." Fox's voice hardened, increasing the pressure. "Who do you work for?"

0397 turned his head away from Fox and the pictures. His shoulders rose up and down with labored breath. "I—I don't know."

"Someone outside the United States gave you those Enhancements and put you up to this attack." Fox's voice raised, pedal on the pressure. "What was it all about? Terrorism directed at the city? The country? Or is this a message for Clover?"

"I—"

Fox slammed his fist over the pictures, his voice booming from his chest. "Who do you work for?"

"I can't remember!" 0397 yelled back. He stood up and

pulled at his restraints. The aluminum chair clanked against the floor.

Fox stood his ground and straightened up, not a single wrinkle in his military suit.

James watched an agitated 0397 engage in a staring match with the commander. He felt the muscles in his crossed arms tense up. 0397's animal instinct activated when he felt threatened. James had experienced it firsthand during his fight with him. He wondered if security would have to intervene or if he'd get to see Commander Fox's abilities in action. A rare spectacle.

0397's restraints wouldn't give way, and the blond's rage cooled off. He lowered his head once more, and the attack dog James fought in the parking garage didn't make an appearance. 0397 looked like a child again, and he was scared.

Fox pulled away. He grabbed his peaked cap from the other end of the table and walked to the heavy metal door. The commander dusted his shoulder while waiting for the door to open with a buzz.

James kept his eyes on the suspect. 0397 lifted his gaze with a curious tilt and focused on a corner of the room. James followed his gaze. What was he looking at? James only saw the empty corner.

"Tiger." Commander Fox's voice made him turn away from the interrogation room.

"Commander." James saluted as Fox walked up, his polished shoes gleaming with the overhead lights.

"Any first thoughts?"

"I wouldn't know, sir. He remembers the Arts District but has no recollection of the attack. He comes from Germany but says he doesn't remember making it to the States. He thinks he might be eighteen years old but doesn't remember his name." James took a deep breath. "It all seems strange."

"And convenient, to say the least."

"Do you think he's lying?"

"Hard to say. Perhaps he believes he's telling the truth."

"Sir?"

"It wouldn't be the first time a GENE loses control and has no recollection of their actions. You said he acted erratic in your encounter, correct?"

"Yes, sir. Komodo and Crimson confirmed as much."

"Enhancements sometimes don't mix well with a subject's mind. Especially when testing new variations."

James thought of all the possible outcomes for 0397 if that were true. At best, he'd end up in the Garden City Facility, where he could enter a rehab program for rogue GENEs. At worst, the company would send him to the Research Center in Hart Island and apply the Exit Clause. The thought gave way to an empty pit in his stomach.

"What will happen to him now?"

Commander Fox took a look at the kid on the other side of the fake wall. "I'll have him tested by the Psychological Department and move our investigation from there."

James rubbed his chin. The intervention from the Psychological Department would cost them at least forty-eight hours on turning in a report. "Sir, how fast do the directors want our mission report?"

"They've already requested we turn in whatever information we have about the mission." The commander shook his head. "I asked them for more time so we could get them a full report in a couple of weeks, but they wouldn't budge. Honey is delivering our briefing and mission transcript as we speak."

James took a second to visualize the transcript the directors would get. Their mission hadn't been especially smooth. He mentally checked off everything the Military Department might consider a mistake. The results didn't look good. James had engaged with an Enhanced suspect and didn't ask for reinforcements until his suspect had escaped him. Robin's venom didn't paralyze the suspect, and she didn't administer the antidote in time. Alyssa created an electrochemical explosion that required extensive cover-up.

James couldn't help but grimace. "Won't the directors find our mission transcript unsatisfactory?"

"Oh, I'm sure they will. Our Unit could do a perfect job, and they would still rummage around for something to be displeased at."

James' mouth went dry. He didn't know what would happen if the directors found the Deltas' performance below average, much less if they were displeased. "What would happen to our Unit, sir?"

"That's uncertain." The commander shook his head. "They could just bench us from Enhanced cases—nothing we haven't come back from. But they could try disbandment again."

With his jaw tensing up, James' thoughts flipped through everything the directors had put the Deltas through that year alone. "Sir, permission to speak frankly."

Fox held his hand out, granting him permission to continue.

"Why are they trying so hard to get rid of us? We're a small Unit. Our station is not prestigious either. And yet, the directors keep making up rules that affect us directly. Like when they announced all units needed to have at least three members by the end of the summer, or else get disbanded and threatened to disband us."

"Finding a third member in such short notice wasn't easy," Fox agreed. "We were lucky to find Crimson's applications among the recently graduated cadets."

"Exactly. They wouldn't allow us to take that new cadet you recruited last year. I know he's young and still undergoing the GENE program, but other units used recruits in training to fill their spots. Why couldn't we?" James shook his head. "I don't get it."

Fox exhaled, seeming to weigh his response. "This conversation never happened, understand?"

James' stomach did a somersault. Why the sudden secrecy? "Yes, sir."

"Very well." The commander nodded. "I'm sure you've heard about the Enhanced People's Rights Movement."

"I have, in passing."

"Do you know for how long the movement has been around, Tiger?"

James blinked twice. "No, sir." He had suspected Fox was possibly involved with the EPR, but he'd never seen any confirmation of it.

"Thirteen years. And in that time, we had never had a real chance of becoming a real movement." The golden glint in Fox's eyes sharpened just as steel forged under pressure. "The battle for equal rights has never been easy. It's even harder to fight it when we're not even supposed to exist."

An uncomfortable lump grew on the back of his throat. James swallowed.

"We've got a fighting chance this time because of my position as Commander. The department suspects my involvement in the movement but haven't had any proof. I guess that, if they shoot me down, they get to shoot down the EPR, too"

James felt dizzy with all the information and questions swimming in his head. In the end, he was able to only ask one. "How can I help?"

"For now, just focus on the case. The best thing we can do for the movement is to make sure 0397 ends up in the right place. He's a high-profile suspect because of his unique abilities. If we can do what's right for him, we could set a new precedent for Enhanced cases." Fox turned back to the double-way mirror, the outline of his silhouette reflected with sharp and precise lines. "Crimson will be writing the report—I expect you'll guide her in the process."

"You got it, sir."

"Excellent. I'll worry about the directors and whatever they throw at us next. " Fox turned back to James and looked him up and down. "You should go home, James. Get some rest. We're barely getting started."

"Yes, sir." James saluted him again as the Commander made his way out of the Holding Facility.

James turned to 0397 again. The kid sat in silence, still staring at that corner, perhaps lost in thought.

Eighteen.

At that age, James had been rushing to get his high school diploma. He'd dreamed of enlisting into the army like his father. His only worries were about who to take to prom.

This kid could end up seeing the last of his days in a research laboratory, doctors and scientists his only company. The only thing he'd have to look forward to was the Exit Clause: a lethal injection. This sort of scenario was what the EPR movement looked to change. And they had been fighting a losing battle for thirteen years. His stomach turned, acid coating his esophagus.

James stayed with 0397 until the security detail came to sedate and retrieve him.

The first light of day was soft on the horizon, tinting the sky in pastel pinks and blues. The day was young, but James felt nothing like it. He drove through downtown, the streets quiet and almost serene. It was as if nothing had ever happened. Just a few blocks away, the Arts District slept. Later that morning, a news crew would surely report the attack on the Blue Flamingo. They'd leave out any details of Enhanced people being involved, and the GENE secrecy would be safe once again.

James scoffed to himself.

A red light marked a stop for him right in front of City Hall. James took the opportunity to rub his eyes. Funny how the Clover Enhancements made him strong enough to lift up to five tons but not strong enough to resist the weight of his eyelids. He had a couple of miles to go before he'd make it home. The promise of a shower and his bed sounded like a luxury.

When he opened his eyes again, the light was still red. The loud revs of a huge engine from the corner called his attention. The city's Sweeper was doing its regular rounds around City Hall.

With his hands tightening around the steering wheel, James regarded that vehicle with contempt. The armored police car was as black as the shame that settled in his chest. Its walls were made of pure galvanized steel, and it had bulletproof windows. The Sweepers were the legacy of William Wade, New Graysons' Mayor. They were meant to wipe the city clean of crime, or so the campaigns for their funding preached.

Keep our streets stainless Gray. Keep our Sons safe, Mayor Wade's campaign slogans had chanted.

In the end, the Sweepers were used at the Mayor's discretion. After the government announced an Executive Order restricting freedom of speech, Wade used the Sweepers to arrest protestors. When the Supreme Court upheld the order, the Sweepers were used to break up the riots. The Sweepers had called the attention of other cities, and soon, every other city in America had a fleet of armored cars. Seven years later, Wade was still in office, and he used the Sweepers to patrol the city, free of the homeless and kids violating curfew.

James scoffed as he saw the Sweeper disappear behind City

Hall. He hoped they wouldn't find anyone to arrest that night. People knew how dangerous it was to be caught breaking curfew, especially near federal buildings.

It felt like there was rot everywhere—his city, his career, and now his case with 0397. James knew the case would be hard from the start, but he had a feeling things would get even more complicated. Writing the report, for starters, would not be an easy task by any means. He feared then that Fox would be right. The company would do everything to keep them down. Was it all really to get Fox and the EPR officially shut down?

The streetlight turned green. James drove off with a different kind of tiredness strangling his heart.

Cold concrete floor received Miguel as he stepped into the Clover Holding Facility. The sound of his naked feet echoed against the emptiness of the premises. Shadow Braid floated past him, and the door closed behind them with a metallic grunt.

A long corridor of gray concrete walls and industrial floors extended before them. Was that the sound of rain coming from somewhere in the hall? Miguel could not only hear it but also smell it as if he were right under it. A single flickering light bulb illuminated the corridor with an intermittent orange tint.

Miguel saw where the rain was coming from. In the cavernous depths of the facility, the hall transformed into some backstreet's alley. When he looked up, he just saw the roof, dry as could be, but when he looked down, he saw the rain coming down around him, red lightning crackling in his peripheral vision. Miguel looked away. His head hurt as he tried to process more details about the alley. Looking at it strained his eyes as if he were trying to see through a thin, black blindfold.

As he walked, Miguel wondered where the other version of

the detention center existed. What would Clover need to "hold" in the real-life facility?

Miguel stood in front of a window mounted on the wall and examined the black reflective surface. A two-way mirror, like in the US Border Holding Center. This window must lead to an interrogation room.

"These places—" Miguel's voice filled the hall as he looked at the shape of his reflection. "Looks like we are in someone's memories. Is that right?

Shadow Braid stopped in front of the double-way mirror. She shook her head without looking at him.

"Okay, not memories. But my apartment and the compound back there are places we know because we've been there before." Miguel frowned and scratched the side of his head. "Can we only visit places one of us has been at before?"

Shadow Braid's hair floated around her as she nodded.

"Ha!" Miguel snapped his fingers as if he were winning at charades. "Okay, so I have never been in this place. You couldn't get in here earlier, so you haven't either. Does it belong to someone else?"

Shadow Braid turned to him, her movements sluggish. Something was wrong. Her lips were cracked, her gaze dull.

"Are you okay?" Miguel asked, his questions forgotten.

She ignored the question and pointed at the two-way mirror instead. A light turned on, revealing a green-colored room on the other side. A table, two chairs, and several cameras looked like they belonged there. The Chinese doll sitting at a far corner did not.

"How come that doll is everywhere we go?" Miguel continued to analyze the Chinese princess. "Wait..." He strained his eyes to get a better look. "Why is her forehead cracked?"

Shadow Braid made one of those choking sounds as she tried to speak, and then she collapsed to the floor.

"Hey!" Miguel rushed over to Shadow Braid and held the girl in his arms as she shook.

Shadow Braid looked up. The wisps of hair didn't float around her like shadows anymore. For the first time since he'd known her, she looked tired. She looked human.

Miguel's neck tightened, and his head grew heavy with knowledge. Shadow Braid served as the one and only connection between realities. While she was guiding him around this dreamlike reality, she was also holding the pieces of the shadow world together. When he granted them access to the facility, he added a new location to the shadow world. It was proving to be a heavy burden on her. She was like an old computer trying to run one too many applications.

"Maybe we should turn back," Miguel said, helping Shadow Braid back to her feet.

Shadow Braid considered it, her breathing labored with exhaustion. Then she shook her head. With a look, she told Miguel there was something she needed to find in the facility. She held on tight to his arm. In her touch, Miguel felt she needed his help.

It occurred to Miguel that he followed Shadow Braid only to find out whether she was real, and now he was sure of it. She was as real as the places they'd visited. Somewhere outside the shadow world, there was a girl that needed his help. Shadow Braid was only a twisted version of that person.

"Just show me where to go." He put her arm around his shoulders and continued down the hall.

TIGER_

A comfortable warmth filled James after he stretched and indulged in a long yawn. He'd slept a deep and undisturbed sleep for a solid seven hours. Just around four o'clock, he left the velvety comfort of his bedroom in search of a glass of water.

Midday light filtered through the blinds of his living room. The hum of the fish tank filter was the only sound that accompanied his steps to the kitchen. James gulped down a full glass of water and let out a loud and satisfied exhale

In his twenty-five years of life, silence had always been a rarity. Growing up, the sounds of younger siblings in a small home never allowed quiet moments to settle. He'd traded that bustle for the one in the US Army, and soon after, he'd adopted the noises of the Clover facility. The silence in his condo belonged to him.

Turning on the coffee machine, James thought of going by Clover, even though Fox had given him the rest of the day off. He couldn't start working on the case since they had to wait for the Psychological Department to turn in 0397's assessment. But maybe if he just happened to be at the company gym, he could swing by the commander's office and just so happen to find out if the directors sent any feedback about his Unit's performance.

A chirp from the breakfast table called his attention. James found his phone right where he'd left it when he got home that morning. With a swipe of his thumb, he glanced at his notifications. He had two missed calls and three text messages from Robin.

What was she doing calling and texting him? The Medical Department had probably sent her home already, but she should be resting instead of attempting to communicate with him for hours. He read the texts.

Are you up yet? I just heard the Legal Department will be on the news today. Do you know anything about that?

How are you still sleeping? Call me when you see this.

Turn on the 4 pm news when you wake up. Legal will be handling the press release for sure.

His worry bubbling up, James went to the living room and turned on the news.

City Hall appeared on the screen atop his fireplace. The white stone structure stood in the middle of the scene, surrounded by crisp green trees and a multitude of camera crews. Reporters flocked around a podium set just below the steps of City Hall. A red and blue digital strip with the newscast logo ran across the screen. It read, *Blue Flamingo Attack: Mayor Wade and Clover Co. spokesperson speak to the community.* This was the official statement both the government and Clover would release. This was the Blue Flamingo Incident's cover-up.

James typed a reply to Robin and sat on his futon. *I'm watching now.*

Three men stood behind the podium, having a whispered conversation while waiting for New Graysons' Mayor to make an appearance. The first man was the Legal Department viceroy—James would recognize his shining bald head anywhere. Máximo Reyes de la O served as the liaison between the Military and Legal Departments. He held powerful positions in both as the Director of Public Relations and Commander of the Beta Unit. Mister O was a man that advertised his wealth and status from the way he walked to his expensive shoes and designer-cut vests. If James had to put a face to the Enhanced People's Rights Movement's opposition, this man would be the first one to come to mind.

Clapping erupted, and the cameras panned to catch the entrance of a tall and languid man wearing a raven-black suit. Mayor Wade waved for the cameras as he walked to the podium. He shook hands with the men already on the scene. When he pumped Mister O's hand, he also patted his shoulder. After taking his place behind the podium, Mayor Wade waited for an instant before kicking off his speech, striking a leaderly pose for the cameras.

"Last night, tragedy struck our beautiful New Graysons. A still-unknown terrorist group attacked our city with military-grade, Enhanced weaponry. Dozens of our sons and daughters were injured in this heinous attack. Many are still at our Medical District, fighting for their lives."

The Mayor paused to observe the crowd. His face was expressionless, leaving his words alone to deliver his message—a well-mastered political move of his. "Despite how saddened I am to see my citizens as the target of such violence, I am proud of how our city responded to the attack on the Blue Flamingo. I want to thank our police department and first responders for their bravery. I also want to thank our allies at Clover for their invaluable assistance in dealing with this threat."

James' phone chirped in his hands with a text from Robin. *Just another terrorist attack by another non-disclosed terrorist agency. Nothing to see here.*

James scoffed. It was always the same. Clover PR would

craft a story to blame GENE-related crimes on nonspecific terrorist agencies or any groups that opposed the government in an effort to squash any protests against the Mayor and the city. He texted back an eye-rolling emoji.

Mayor Wade concluded his address and had opened the floor for Mister O to speak to the press. It wasn't uncommon for the politicians aware of the GENE secrecy initiative to let Clover staff handle the press. Who better to keep a lie consistent than its manufacturers?

Mister O ascended to the podium, and the cameras zoomed in on him. "Thank you, Mister Mayor." A Spanish lisp and a staccato delivery accompanied his words. "Good afternoon. I'll be answering questions about our company's involvement in responding to the Blue Flamingo attack. Before we get started, Clover extends its deepest condolences about last night's occurrences. We ask that the community lend its strength to all the victims. May they win their battle against the injuries suffered and return safely home."

James' face screwed with bitterness as Mister O delivered his message. All the words were right, but no emotion reached his deep hazel eyes. Instead, those eyes sported the confidence of someone who knew they're ahead of the race.

Mister O opened the floor for questioning. The crowd of reporters buzzed rampantly, lifting their recording devices and electronic pads in the air. O picked reporters seemingly at random, but he knew which news representatives would ask the safest questions. James had heard Mister O give the same responses for prior incidents. The attack had been performed by a nondescript group of suspects who belonged to a new terrorist group. They didn't have more details about the suspects or their organization since they were still under investigation. Clover claimed jurisdiction of the case because the use of Enhanced weaponry was confirmed. The media pushed for further clarification, and Mister O took the opportunity to remind everyone that Clover was the worldwide leader in Defense Research.

Mister O announced they had time for just a couple more questions and a voice lifted above all others. "Excuse me!"

James squinted to catch the sight of a brunette in glasses elbowing her way to the front of the crowd. "Excuse me, Mister O. Parker Laney, for *The Conspirator's Log*." The woman lifted a pen in the air to call Mister O's attention.

For a fraction of a second, Mister O scanned the security fences placed around City Hall, perhaps wondering who had let this woman in. The name of the media outlet the woman shouted out didn't promise inoffensive questions like the ones from the *Times* or the *Gray Harbinger*. In the end, Mister O pointed at her like he had done for all the other reporters.

"Mister O, do you have a statement about the allegations that the person responsible for the attack was a Refurbished Human and not a terrorist organization?"

The flock of reporters went silent. James shifted in his seat; a sudden wave of cold ran down his spine. He'd heard that term before. Every now and then, conspiracy theorists would manage to stay afloat through smaller media outlets. Among theories about lizard people and Bigfoot, whispers of superhuman soldiers floated around. The theory claimed the government enlisted alien hybrids in their service. The general public didn't know about GENEs, but the conspiracy theorists had dubbed them "Refurbished Humans."

Discreet giggles spread around the flock of reporters and newscasters. Allegations like this one were still seen as a big joke, even though Parker Laney was unknowingly veering too close to illegal information distribution. Big media outlets discredited magazines like the one Parker Laney worked for. Free press restrictions ensured that their reach was stifled.

104 / MICHELLE MONÁRREZ

James was sure this would be the first and last time he'd hear about *The Conspirator's Log*.

"Miss Laney, was it?" Mister O coughed into his fist as if trying to stifle a chortle. "No, Clover has no comment about any Refurbished Humans. Our company is concerned with being your main provider of technological, medical, and energy advancements. Our mission is still to deliver research that would rebuild and enhance every nation through our study of post-war technology. No further questions."

And just like that, the GENE secrecy was safe again. From the back of his head, Fox's words came back to him: *The battle for equal rights has never been easy. It's even harder to fight it when we're not even supposed to exist.* James turned off the television, scowling.

For the last two years, he'd worked hard to keep his Unit together. He obeyed orders. He didn't ask questions. And it had all been to protect the GENE secrecy. Was this really the right thing to do?

The company stated that keeping GENEs secret was for the better. The public wasn't ready to know about them. But this only meant that GENEs had no one backing them up. If the company decided that writing off 0397 as a mental case and having him killed by researchers was best for the GENE secrecy, would it be his place to let it happen?

As if someone had flipped a switch inside him, James refused to let it happen.

It no longer felt right to protect this secret above everything else. The people he was to protect should include rogue GENEs as well. Even with all their Enhancements and all their malfunctions, they were still human.

He could do more. He could get involved in the Enhanced People's Rights Movement.

James paused as he thought of his Unit. If the directors

knew both the Commander and Unit Leader were involved in Enhanced Rights, they would become a bigger target. Was it fair to put both Robin and Alyssa's careers on the line? He'd need advice from someone with keener political sensibilities. And he needed his Unit's buy-in.

His phone rang with a call from Robin. James made up his mind before answering. He wouldn't be stopping by Clover that day after all.

By the time he made it to the Bluevue Estate, the sun was already hiding behind the horizon. The drive up Bluevue Mountain led past homes customized to match the capricious land. The properties displayed bigger and more intricate designs the higher they sat on the mountain.

Robin's house sat on the highest ring of homes. As far as James knew, the lavish home came to her as an inheritance, which she maintained now with her own career at Clover. The home was styled in modern architecture, lush gardens, and a polished stone driveway matched Robin to perfection. A sharp mind with excellent taste.

James parked his car in his regular spot and crossed the snowy gardens. A woman in a housekeeping uniform greeted him at the door. He followed her inside the home and was asked to wait in the foyer.

"James!" A young man carrying a tray with assorted empty bowls and syringes walked down the stairs. The navy blue scrubs with the Clover logo printed on them identified him as a company nurse.

"Louis Adrieux," James said with a smile, and he shook the nurse's hand. He knew Louis as Robin's preferred nurse for when she had to stay home and recover from using her abilities.

"How've you been? It's been a while."

"Too long, man. I see Robin has you up to taking care of her again. My sympathies." James knew from being her partner that Robin wasn't an easy patient.

Louis chuckled, and James knew half of that was in agreement.

"Is she up to any visitors? I asked earlier if I could stop by, but I know it's getting late."

Louis tossed his hand up. "Oh, don't worry about the time. She's not sleeping, if that's what you're worried about. Being up to visitors might be a different matter."

"Is she not feeling well?"

Louis gave him a pained smile. "She's not in a good mood."

James followed Louis up the stairs and through the main hall. It overlooked the pool and the greenhouse on the back patio. Normally, James wouldn't have even rung the doorbell; he would have walked straight to the greenhouse where Robin spent most of her time. She often said she preferred the company of snowdrops, the veratrum, and belladonna lilies to other people.

With a knock on the open bedroom door, Louis made their presence known.

"What is it?" Robin spoke without looking up the electronic tablet she was reading from, her voice tinged with an extra note of irritation.

"James Kings is here to see you, Miss Night."

A bittersweet smile spread on Robin's face. "Well, well. Took you long enough." She pointed at a chair close to her bed. "Come in, have a seat."

James took his spot next to Robin. He hadn't seen her since he took her to Clover's Medical Wing and the doctors shooed him away. Looking at his partner up close, he realized how much the use of her abilities had taken out of her. Her skin looked as brittle as onion skin paper, and he could see the many fine purple veins branching out from the corner of her hands.

"Louis, would you be so kind as to bring me a cup of tea?"

"What kind, Miss Night?"

"Make it chamomile and lavender with three spoonfuls of honey, but not the one we keep in the guest's cupboard. Ask Jessica where we keep the good honey."

Louis smirked. "Yes, Miss Night. Anything else?"

"James?" Robin offered.

"Just a glass of water, thanks." James gave the nurse a grateful smile.

Robin waited until Louis was gone to speak again.

"Isn't he just what the doctor ordered?" Robin said with a purr. "He doesn't give me sass like the rest of them. He's quick, he's cheerful, he's...perky..."

James ignored her comments and examined the dark rings around her eyes and the many noncorrosive bandages around her hand. She moved her silvery hair out of her face and smiled at him.

"Oh, please don't give me that look. You know how it is. Sometimes I get a little crazy, but it's nothing a simple transfusion can't fix."

"Someone could have died the other night, Robin."

She waved a hand in front of her face. "Spare me the lecture, will you? Your boss has already given me one."

"What? When?"

Robin signaled to a pink sheet sitting on the nightstand. "That lovely letter was waiting for me when I got home. Apparently, Fox had Honey drop it off while I was at the hospital. It's not the get-well card I was expecting."

James took the paper and read on. "A disciplinary leave. For how long?"

"Three weeks. Can you believe it? What am I supposed to do with myself for three weeks?" She scoffed out a laugh. "And as if the suspension wasn't enough, this will go on my permanent record."

James let a low whistle escape. This had to be coming from the directors. "Fox said the directors asked him to deliver everything we had on the case last night, including our mission transcript."

Robin took a moment to process his words. "That explains it, then. I guess someone had to take the fall for the mistakes we made. It couldn't be you because you're the Unit Leader. It couldn't be Alyssa because she's already had marks on her record. That leaves me."

James grimaced. He didn't expect these kinds of consequences. His leading position protected him this time, but his delay on calling reinforcements could have him on disciplinary leave just as well. Alyssa's GENE clearance going wrong could have at least sentenced her to an extended stay in the Records Room. As far as he was concerned, Robin had done everything according to the Military Handbook. "That's not fair."

"Politics are a dirty bitch." She shrugged. "I'll be fine. Fox knows Jim Rogers has a soft spot for me. Maybe I'll casually mention the mark on my record and he'll do something about it."

James snickered. It was true. The Co-Director of the Military Department had been a longtime friend of Robin's adoptive father. He'd aided the Deltas before out of his appreciation for her. "How you ever managed to stay on Roger's good side is beyond me."

"He was a bit ticked off when I signed to work for Fox. He and Father called it career suicide, but I'm too charming to stay mad at." Robin's mouth curled up in a smile as if she'd suddenly remembered something amusing. "So, there was something you wanted to talk to me about. What is it?"

James took a deep breath. He looked over his shoulder to double-check they were still alone. "It's about the Enhanced People's Rights Movement. Fox's in pretty deep, and I want to join him, but I don't feel right about doing it before talking to you and Alyssa. If I join, that could affect your careers. I'd help you change units, if you want."

Robin blinked. She studied him, absorbing his words. When she spoke, her words came out slow and measured. "Okay. I'll join, too"

"Really?" He gaped. "You will?"

"You know, if Fox is as deep in as you say, we've already been associated with it. I might as well do something good for a change." She shrugged like she had just decided to have dessert before dinner.

"This is great, Robin." James smiled, relieved. "I'm so glad you're joining me on this."

"Yeah, yeah, relax." Robin waved a hand in front of her and looked away. "It's no big deal."

"I'm just saying." He laughed. "We've been working together for so long. I guess it would've been weird to do this without you."

"Ugh, you're so corny." She turned back to him after rolling her eyes. "Are you sure we can trust Alyssa? I mean, kid's great and all, but she's been with us for three months."

Robin's comment gave him pause. Three months was a short time to talk about something like this in confidence. But Alyssa was the kind of soldier that didn't always play by the rules. She had, after all, continued to solve those Enhanced Narcotic cases while she worked at the Records Room. "I think we can."

"You think?" She raised an eyebrow. "Well, you gotta be

sure before bringing her in. We shouldn't take any chances with this."

James knew he couldn't blame Robin for being so mistrusting. Her amethyst eyes had a shine that spoke of a sharp wit and insight beyond her twenty-four years. Being born inside Clover's GENE program would give you that.

"You're right," James said. "I'll make sure we can trust her before I mention it to her."

Robin nodded. She stared into his eyes, lost in thought. "James, we've seen these kinds of cases before. Why the sudden need to support the movement?"

Leaning in, James rested his forearms over his lap. He told her everything about Fox's place within the movement and how protecting the GENE secrecy didn't feel right anymore. James spoke of how helping 0397 get the right verdict from the directors might help the movement, though it would be challenging.

"It's all pretty strange," James said after concluding his retelling of the interview. "The kid has no name or remembrance of the attack. He was only able to tell us that he's from Germany and, well... that much was obvious."

"He could be faking," Robin mused. "Although the kid looked pretty crazy already."

"Fox thought so, too. He said he'd bring in the Psychological Department."

"The shrinks' involvement always delays an investigation. I wonder why the directors are so keen on getting all the information they can already." Robin's purple eyes shone with an alertness that wasn't there before. "Unless the directors are getting pressed by someone else to deliver a preliminary verdict."

James looked at her, not really sure what she meant. Robin had this sixth sense for politics and was pretty good at guessing what games the higher-ups were playing.

She seemed to sense his confusion. "You're worried about the directors."

"I am. It wouldn't be the first time the directors send a rogue GENE to Hart Island without even seeing a full report." James pinched the bridge of his nose. "They shouldn't be able to do that."

"They shouldn't," Robin agreed. "But I don't think they will this time. The company would never send someone like him away. Not even if the assessment is negative."

"What do you mean?" James was lost again.

Robin snickered as if she had an inside joke with someone else and found it endearing he wasn't in on it. "When was the last time you saw something like what the kid has instead of an arm?"

James shook his head in response.

"Exactly. Fox hadn't seen anything like it, and people in the department probably haven't either. That means this might be a new type of variation, and the company would want to capitalize on this."

"But what about the incident?" As soon as the question left his lips, James realized how gullible he'd sounded.

Robin turned to him with a condescending smile. "The company couldn't give two shits about the incident. That kid's a weapon, and weapons are assets."

A lyssa cringed at the mess at her workstation. Stained coffee mugs hid in piles behind her monitors. Small mountains of paper balls loitered around the keyboard. She lost track of how many hours she'd spent at Tactical trying to piece together any clues for the case.

At first, she thought writing a black and white report of the events involving 0397 should be easy. That was, until their suspect claimed he couldn't remember the attack on the Blue Flamingo or much of who he was. Whether that was true or not, she now had to construct his account of the events. Fox gave her security videos from law enforcement to work with and nothing else, and she had to present them to the Military Department's directors along with her written report. They'd decide what to do with Suspect 0397 then.

As far as what that would be, she wasn't sure. They could send him to the Garden City Facility in Colorado. Rogues like him could turn their lives around after some time at Clover's correctional branch. Not that she should be worrying about it. Her job was still to present the facts. No more, no less.

Alyssa sat back down at her workstation. She swiped the

paper balls away from her keyboard. The digital calendar marked the date as November 24. She still had ten days to deliver her report. Plenty of time. Except that the Deltas had nothing to show for the work put in over the last three days, not even with James helping her.

Her heart beating faster than before, she turned her monitors on and pulled a new report form. She opened the list of the videos she had arranged in chronological order. Alyssa paused, noticing a field she hadn't before. Under the legend *Unit Recommendation* there was a tiny box for comments from the reporter.

Alyssa snorted. Like someone would care about what the Fixed Foxes had to say.

She hit play on her videos.

The sequence started with the video from an ATM in front of the Blue Flamingo. A flash of dirty yellow hair appeared on the screen. In the awful resolution from the ATM camera, 0397 played the part of someone who shouldn't have been in the Arts District. He stood out like a crack on the daintiest china with his swaying walk and dirty clothes. He looked dazed, lost.

The medical examination on 0397 reported undernourishment and dehydration. Did his hunger prevent him from thinking clearly, and he ended up in the Arts District by accident? After seeing him in the videos, it was clearly not a terrorist attack.

For the hundredth time, Alyssa started the video that she believed showed the catalyst of the Blue Flamingo Incident. A red convertible slowed down next to 0397 and followed him for a few strides. One of the passengers threw what looked like a styrofoam cup at him. Orange, icy liquid splattered out of the cup and smeared over 0397's clothes. The convertible drove off and disappeared behind the valet parking of the Blue Flamingo, abandoning her suspect. 0397 looked down at his jacket, took it off, and assessed the damage. The next time he looked up, he stared at the direction his attackers had gone. He held the jacket in his hands, and glared at the busy streets leading to the Blue Flamingo Club for a long while without moving a muscle.

Alyssa bit her thumbnail as she watched 0397 break from his spell and walk up to the Blue Flamingo. She paused the video as if she could pause that moment and hold 0397 from continuing on his path. He wanted to make them pay for the insult, the mockery, and his ruined jacket. If Alyssa didn't know what he'd done that night, she would've cheered him on.

Keep it together, Dietrich, she told herself. *You're supposed to stay neutral.*

She hit play on the video again. 0397 made his way to the Blue Flamingo at 12:15 am, November 18.

Alyssa left Tactical with her stomach screaming at her. The time she'd been spending with videos of 0397 was far from healthy. A quiet meal away from her monitors might help with her thoughts about siding with possible terrorists.

She sat down in front of a meal of eggs, sausage, and tea. Clover had a so-called wide selection of teas. Alyssa suspected they were all the same kind—a weak blend of dried up leaves— with different labels. But she'd take it over nothing.

Nothing could compare with the British branch's tea, resources, and the respect GENEs got over there.

Alyssa's chest ached with nostalgia.

When she left England, she never imagined she'd miss home this much. Alyssa had never been one to cry, but some- times she felt like it when it rained. The smell of earth soaking the cold rain and the sights of colorful umbrellas made her think of London. She thought of the childhood afternoons she spent in a wheelchair, parked next to the bay windows in the banquet room. While the nerves in her spine and legs recovered from the Clover Enhancement Process, the rest of the neighborhood children played in the rain. The sound of her caretaker, Dudley, playing the piano filtered through bittersweet memories. Gentle notes danced from his fingertips when her legs couldn't. It wasn't London she missed, she realized then. It was the man who took care of her during her weakest moments.

Allowing herself a wistful smile, she picked up her styrofoam cup of American tea.

"It's no cup of builder's, but it'll have to do," she whispered to herself before taking in the first sip. She managed to not make a face when the scalding, bitter drink swirled around her mouth.

Alyssa glanced up and spotted a familiar lean shape at the cafeteria's register. Her stomach went cold.

It could be a mistake, she tried to convince herself. No luck. The flip of the head to remove his bangs from his eyes and the crystalline laugh were unmistakable. Esteban Tomassetti, the Beta Unit Leader, tried to decide whether to have milk or orange juice.

She met Esteban before she moved to the States. He'd been a guest at her home branch, and her superiors bestowed upon her the task of guiding him around the city for over a week.

Ever since she moved to America, Alyssa worried she'd run into the smooth Italian guy. Alyssa couldn't put her finger on it. Maybe it was the charming smile he gave her or the inviting spark in his deep golden eyes. Perhaps it was the discreet softness of his Florentine accent when he spoke. Alyssa couldn't put her finger on it, but she just hated the guy.

Alyssa caught herself glaring as Esteban's joke had the cashier giggling like a bloody idiot. She rolled her eyes and decided to take her breakfast back at Tactical. She stood up with her tray and, by sheer coincidence, Esteban looked in her direction. Her fiery hair as red as the electricity cruising through her veins didn't help her go unnoticed.

So much for having a quiet meal.

When she saw the spark of recognition on Esteban's face, she put her tray down and forced her face to form a tiny smile.

"Well, I'll be damned. The Crimson Thunder in the States?" Esteban approached her, holding a box of orange juice in his hand.

Alyssa wanted to vanish right then. She wished she stayed at Tactical. She motioned to salute him, as his rank surpassed her own.

"Don't be so formal, Alyssa." Esteban raised a hand. "Relax."

Alyssa tried to smile again. "Hi, Esteban."

"I heard you'd been transferred. I kept wondering if I'd see you around."

"Yeah. I've been here for a couple of months now."

Esteban sat down and invited Alyssa to do the same as if she was the one that had interrupted his breakfast. "How long will we have you with us?"

"Eighteen months." Her hopeless tone was far more palpable than she would have liked.

"Wow. That bad, huh?"

"I beg your pardon?"

"Rumor has it you got transferred for disciplinary reasons." He emphasized the last words with air quotes. "Eighteen months away from your Unit means you were pretty... naughty."

Alyssa felt her jaw clench, and her face grew hot. She gave a thin smile. "Well, rumors are just that. I requested the transfer myself to expand my career."

"In eighteen months?"

"It's just a trial period. I'm hoping to stay." She was

impressed at how lies flowed out of her. And how she'd managed to not punch him yet.

"Really? What an interesting change in careers! I would have never traded the prestige you had with the Enhanced Task Forces. What was your Unit going to be called? The Light Bearers?"

Alyssa's face was on fire, and she wondered for how much longer she could be polite. The name of her old Unit on his lips hurt in her chest. She swallowed hard. "Yes, it would have been a Unit under Enhanced Narcotics, but I decided to explore other career options."

Esteban gave her a little smile and a wink. "In that case, welcome to the American branch."

"Thank you." Alyssa took a sip of her now lukewarm tea.

"Well, since you are looking to grow your career, let me give you a word of advice."

Alyssa managed to keep her face straight as Esteban talked. She didn't want the guy close to her, much less his advice. He started off by explaining how he'd been around her age when he started working for the company. It'd taken him two years to become the Unit Leader for the Betas, the elite in Clover's private army.

"So, you see, I'm barely twenty and already have a career many envy. But it's all about knowing the right people. Who are you working with now?"

"I'm with the Delta Unit."

Esteban made a face as if what she said had hurt him. "With Fox? That's too bad. You'll want to ditch the Deltas soon."

"Is that so?"

"Hey, nothing against Tiger and Komodo." He chortled. "They're great, worked with them a couple of times on larger assignments. Fox is the real issue here."

"Why do you say that?"

"The guy doesn't seem to be a bad Commander, if I'm honest." Esteban shrugged. "But he sucks at playing ball with the other biggies, you know?"

Alyssa felt her mouth twist in a frown. Fox was a bad political player. He didn't kiss enough ass. He didn't ask for favors, so he didn't owe anyone anything. None of that concerned her. She preferred honesty and integrity rather than some sleaze bag at the front of her Unit.

"If I were in your shoes, I'd use any case to get the attention of other commanders. What are you working on right now?"

"We are processing this GENE we picked up a few days ago."

Esteban took a sip from this juice for the first time since he sat with her. "What's your role in the case?"

Alyssa's annoyance transformed into suspicion with every passing minute. Esteban had stuck with her longer than he should have. "I'm writing the report."

Esteban nodded as if he was trying hard to give two shits about her answer. "Wait, that wouldn't be the case Public Relations had to cover up last weekend? The one at the Arts District?"

Alyssa squinted at his questions. He was interrogating her, disguising the whole thing as a friendly catch-up. She didn't answer. Esteban continued his performance without her.

"I've heard some very interesting things about it. Oh, that case can make all the difference for you."

"Really?"

"Oh, yeah! It's in everyone's mouth now. The bigger units are showing a lot of interest. I've heard he's some kind of Enhanced cyborg—and some kind of nutcase." He laughed. "It'll be a sad day when those abilities get wasted on Hart Island."

Esteban's words felt like a blow to the gut. How did he know all this? No information had been given out yet to the rest of the Military Department. The only ones to know about the cases' details were the Deltas and the Department Directors.

"You know what else is sad?" Esteban leaned in closer, so close that Alyssa caught a whiff of chlorine on him and noticed his hair was still damp from the pool. He had a killer look in his golden eyes, like a cheetah waiting to sprint after its prey. "To know that such a talented soldier as you is getting wasted in the Delta Unit. If you really wanted to advance your career, you should come and work for me."

The smell of chlorine burned at the back of her throat. Her jaw tensed.

"If you sign with my Unit now, after eighteen months, you could choose any career path you want. With my boss' recommendation, Enhanced Narcotics would take you back in a heartbeat." His cunning smirk announced that he had the power to make every promise a reality. "Just show me your report."

From the moment Enhanced Narcotics had rejected her, Alyssa had fantasized about an opportunity to go back. The flutter in her stomach told her, in that moment, why she had spent all that time trying to solve the Bright Stone cases. She didn't just want to keep her investigative muscle flexed. She had wanted her old division to notice her and take her back.

"I can see you might need some time to think about it." Esteban flipped his midnight black hair from his eyes. "Don't take too long."

Esteban stood up from his seat, and Alyssa followed his fluid movements with her eyes.

"If you truly are serious about advancing your career, meet me at the Records Room in an hour." After winking a golden eye, Esteban walked away, leaving her staring at his unfinished juice box.

Back at Tactical, Alyssa sat at her workstation, attempting to work through her assignment. The video of Fox's interrogation of 0397 played on her floating monitor, but she couldn't focus on it.

She stared instead at the clock in the corner of her screen, watching the minutes go by. Esteban had given her an hour to meet him. It felt like she had been trying to decide for longer. She still had twenty minutes left. The Delta Tactical Room was empty—she could just take her paperwork and slip out. It would take her two minutes to go down to the Records Room. There was a short elevator trip between her and the promise of getting her old life back. But was that really what she wanted?

Nausea welled inside her. Alyssa replayed the conversation in her head. In all her time dreaming about a triumphant return to England, she never imagined an opportunity would present itself like this. What would it mean for the Deltas if she took Esteban up on his offer? How much would her betrayal cost them?

Esteban knew too much information about the case and about her—that couldn't come from rumors and the like. Someone had given him what he needed to sway her. Her loyalty to Commander Fox and the Delta Unit was valuable to someone else, but she couldn't figure out why.

Alyssa sat up in her chair. A crawling thought itched at the back of her brain. It was something Esteban had said. He'd spoken of 0397 going to Hart Island as if he were certain of this outcome, even though the directors hadn't announced their verdict. Perhaps he was so certain of this because he knew he'd be able to tempt her. Her betrayal of her Unit would change the Blue Flamingo Incident's outcome. It would condemn 0397 to die at Clover's research facility.

The recorded sound of Fox slamming his fist over the metal table in the interview filled the Delta Tactical Room. She jumped in her chair when he yelled over the speakers of her computer.

"Who do you work for?"

"I can't remember!" 0397's voice also boomed over the speakers.

Alyssa heard his voice in German and paused the video as it filtered through her translator in English. She understood him twice. She believed him twice.

Alyssa peered at the time on the corner of her monitor as another minute went by. She exhaled.

If she ever went back to the UK branch, it would be for her merit and out of her own effort. She had a Unit in America that counted on her, and she wasn't about to let them down. Esteban would be disappointed.

Alyssa pulled her report form back up. She didn't know what the consequences for skipping on Esteban's under-the-table offer would be. Her attention latched back onto the words "Unit Recommendation." She didn't know if writing in that box would mean anything for the directors, but it meant something for her. It meant that, for the first time since she got to the States, she didn't want to keep her head down.

She clicked over the box and started typing.

Miguel half carried, half dragged Shadow Braid through the Clover Holding Facility until they reached a heavy metal door they recognized. It led to the interrogation room. They'd seen it before through the two-way mirror.

He glanced over once more to check on her state. Her skin was cold, her hair dull, and the wisps of shadows didn't float around her like before. His chest stung, pressing him to hurry. He maneuvered her weight to swipe his Clover ID card over the door's reader.

The door granted them access with a beep.

Blinding white light showered the hall. Miguel looked away, surprised by the sudden brightness. Whatever waited for them past that door wasn't the interrogation room from before. They were leaving the Holding Facility and entering a new place—and it was much larger than the room they'd seen before.

White hexagonal panels mounted on the walls illuminated the room with cool, blinding light. The floor's polished white tiles looked almost liquid when the light reflected on them.

Miguel's own shape also stretched across the reflective floor. The panels made Miguel imagine a beehive made of pure light.

An exceptional layer of silence coated the walls of the room. Miguel had never experienced such absence of noise. The whole room gave him a sense of separation. He didn't belong there. Nothing human should be in this white room.

Miguel helped Shadow Braid into the new, luminescent space, trying not to drag her. He jumped when the door slammed behind them.

"Hey," he whispered to Shadow Braid. "We're here."

Miguel waited for a movement of the head or a stone-white finger that would tell him what to do next. Nothing. Shadow Braid clung to his shoulders, limp, like a life-sized doll. He looked around the room for answers. He found only the bright panels mounted on the walls and that deep, eerie silence. Miguel crouched down near a corner and helped Shadow Braid sit against a wall. She slept, her breaths slow, her skin clammy.

"What's wrong with her?" A raspy voice startled him from behind.

Miguel turned around, disoriented. A lanky, blond guy wearing a navy jumpsuit stood in front of him. Had he been in there all this time? The room had been empty before. Miguel searched his face, trying to figure him out. He looked too normal to belong here.

Miguel straightened, guarded. "Where'd you come from?"

The blond made a face as if trying to answer the question caused him a great deal of pain. "I don't know. I've been stuck in this room for a while, and I need to get out of here. You should do the same."

"Stuck? If you want to get out, why not use the door?"

"What door?"

Miguel looked around. The door they used to come in was

gone. All four walls of the room had nothing but bright panels mounted on them. They were all trapped in there now.

Miguel rolled his eyes and exhaled. "This whole reality-bending is getting old."

"Huh?" The blond took a long look at him and then at Shadow Braid. There was a spark of recognition in his eyes. "Wait, I know her."

"You do?"

"Yeah, I saw her before. I thought I was imagining things, with the anesthesia and all." The blond paused as if trying to catch memories from deep inside his mind. "I saw her again a couple of nights ago. I thought it was a dream."

Miguel felt relief from the blond's words. He wasn't the only one seeing Shadow Braid in dreams. Nothing was wrong with him or with his Enhancements.

"Is this a dream too?"

Miguel let out a small sigh, still full of relief. "No."

"Then what is it?"

"I'm not sure." He shrugged. "Maybe another world."

The blond frowned, not believing him. "And where did you come from, then?"

"We were looking for something." Miguel searched for the right answer in his mind. "I think we were looking for you." How did he know these things all of a sudden? Was Shadow Braid still putting information inside his head?

"Me?"

Miguel's neck tightened. He rubbed the tension away while figuring out how to phrase his explanation. "She's been sick since we got here. I think she needed someone else to help her. It's hard to say. She doesn't talk much."

The guy crossed his arms over his chest. He'd rolled up the sleeves of his jumpsuit, showing what looked like a cyborg arm.

The machine attached to his body shined as much as the polished floor tiles. Was he Enhanced?

The blond rearranged his posture, covering his cyborg arm under his human one. Miguel lifted his gaze to look at his face, realizing then he must've been gawking.

"In case you haven't noticed, I'm in a bit of a situation myself." The guy gestured to his outfit, his lips pressed together in a grimace. "You really think I can help?"

For the first time, Miguel noticed his jumpsuit was like the ones they gave in prisons. Did Clover have a prison for Enhanced people? He forced himself to focus on the blond's question. "Well, yeah." Miguel's head hurt, the heavy feeling of borrowed knowledge pressing into his temples. "Why else would we be in a place only you remember?"

"These are my memories?"

"Uh, something like that. We can only visit places we have been to before. This place is yours."

The guy took a step back and scoffed. "Man, this cannot be real," the blond said while looking around. "The guards put me under sedatives; this has to be some crazy dream."

"We're not dreaming, either." Miguel's statement left his mouth with more conviction than he expected. It was like someone else was pushing information out of him.

"How can we be in my memories? I don't remember this place. Then again, I remember so little these days..." The guy stopped as if considering it. "If this isn't a dream, then we shouldn't be here."

"Why? What happens here?"

The blond made the same face full of pain again, and apprehension rode on his voice. "I have a bad feeling about this place but can't remember why." In the end, he put his hands up, renouncing his ideas and Miguel's words. "No. No, this is too crazy. It has to be a dream."

Miguel fought the urge to roll his eyes. "Yeah, whatever. Sometimes you have to go with crazy to find out what's happening."

"And what would that be?"

Miguel bit his thumb. "I think she's making all of this happen. This world or whatever it is, she's connected to it."

"And how do you know all this?"

"I know because she puts it in my head. Ever since I followed her into this world, sometimes I just know things."

The guy stared at him and raised a single, incredulous eyebrow.

"Agh! I don't know how to say it." Miguel groaned, throwing his head back in frustration. Why did he have to explain things when he didn't get them himself? "All of this is real, and she needs our help, okay?"

A choking grunt interrupted them. Miguel turned, worry stinging his chest again. He found Shadow Braid motioning to him. He crouched and held her hand, her skin like wax paper.

"Is she okay?" the blond said behind him.

"I don't know. She can't tell us what's wrong." Miguel turned to the blond. "This is why we were rushing here. She started feeling sick before and insisted we keep going. All this time, it's like she's been looking for something. And then we found you."

"This is impossible," the blond muttered. "I just want to get out of here." He ran the metallic hand through his hair, moving strands off his face. "Even if all of this is real, how can I help her? Or you? I can't even remember my name to help myself."

Shadow Braid gripped Miguel hard and wheezed. She looked at him, her dark eyes urging him to say something.

Miguel's mind flooded with murky waters as he tried to decipher the message. "She's saying that's why we need you."

Shadow Braid nodded.

"Even if this is a dream, what's the harm in helping us?" Miguel continued when he noticed the blond still looked unsure. "It's not like you can get out of here on your own. She controls these realities, so she can get us out."

"You can do that?" the blond asked Shadow Braid.

A loud hum interrupted them before she could gather enough strength to answer. The room shook all around them, and the humming intensified. It reminded Miguel of the radiation chamber and its horrible whirring sounds. It was as if some mechanism was churning somewhere behind those hexagonal panels. His heart jumped to his throat.

"What's happening?" Miguel yelled over the loud hum.

The blond turned to him, primal fear written all over his face. "Nothing good! This is why I told you we needed to get out of here."

"Can we stop it?"

"How would I know?!"

Shadow Braid extended her free hand towards the blond and gripped Miguel's tighter.

The blond looked at her hand as if he could understand, just like Miguel could, what she meant.

"If I help you, can you stop this?" He yelled over the humming as the surrounding lights became brighter. "Can you get us out of here?"

Shadow Braid opened her hand wider with urgency and nodded.

The blond crouched next to them and held hands with Shadow Braid and Miguel. Shadow Braid closed her eyes. Her head hung limp.

"That's it?" the blond said. "We just have to hold hands?"

"I don't think it'll be that easy."

When Shadow Braid lifted her head again, blue light glowed from her eyes. The hue reminded Miguel of the jellyfish dying ashore when he first met her. A live energy came out from Shadow Braid and into him. Miguel felt it pulsating inside him, filling him with adrenaline and charging him up.

The pain didn't come all at once. It started slow and increased with every passing second, like during radiation sessions. Miguel's pulse skyrocketed. A ringing in his ears told him he needed to let go of the energy. It crackled out of him as a bright orange thunderbolt. His body shook, and he heard the blond scream next to him.

Images rushed all around him. Memories pierced his mind as he heard himself cry out.

In the dirt roads of San Gerónimo, the town's square went up in flames. He watched a final riot breaking and held his sister's hand as she cried.

Somewhere in the backstreets of Beijing, a man counted a fat bundle of bills. He climbed on the back of a government van, renouncing his old life.

The cold alleys of Bavaria served as his refuge. He shivered as he hid from the army's armored trucks, trying his best to cover up his right arm.

They were a blank slate. Memories of snowy forests in Germany swirled somewhere in their heads as they ran, unable to catch up. Their name was unknown.

They were a young girl in China. The mission of serving their country served as a mantra as they endured procedures and radiation. Their name was Daiyu.

They were a Chilean refugee. The Mexican desert extended for miles, marking the long voyage ahead. They cowered against their father's chest. Their name was Miguel.

TIGER_

U nit *Recommendation: Suspect 0397 exhibits the symptoms of memory loss regarding personal identity, personal history, and the events of the Blue Flamingo Incident. According to a psychological evaluation, the suspect is suffering from a dissociative fugue. Further research is pending to assess whether the state is reversible. Due to these results and further evidence in the Suspect's behavior, this Unit is recommending that Suspect 0397 is sent to the rehabilitation program at Garden City Facility.*

James read the printout of the mission report Alyssa had written last night. She had printed out her work in crisp, thick paper and placed it inside an elegant manilla folder. The report form was accompanied by notes from the suspect interview, citations from both the medical and psychological assessments, and a complex timeline detailing the events of November 18. To say that Alyssa had gone above and beyond to produce an excellent report was an understatement.

An easy smile ran across his face as he read the Unit Recommendation again. Fox had tasked him with aiding Alyssa, but she had hardly needed him. She had even gone further than he would have suggested. Unit Recommendations weren't that common. They were seen as a way to try to influence the Directors' decision on a case.

When Robin asked him if they could trust Alyssa with the Enhanced People's Rights Movement, James wasn't sure. After reading her report, Unit Recommendation and all, he was sure.

The door of their tactical office opened with a soft puff. Alyssa entered the Tactical Room carrying two coffees and a brown paper bag. She'd been looming anxiously over his shoulder while he read, so he'd told her to take a break and get them both some coffee. Alyssa placed the grease-stained bag on his desk, the smell of sausage and biscuits escaping its insides. James hadn't asked for food, but the sudden smell made his stomach rumble.

"So? How is it?" Alyssa asked as she plopped on the desk next to his.

James put the papers down and took a sip of the coffee she'd brought. With the bitter taste of Colombian roasted beans swirling in his mouth, he smiled as he turned to her. "Not bad."

Alyssa reached for her own coffee. "But?"

"No buts." He took the breakfast he hadn't known he needed. "You've done your research, and it shows. I especially liked the Unit Recommendation bit."

Alyssa hid her face behind her paper coffee cup. "I wasn't sure if I should write it at all."

"It works. If I'm honest, I would have probably written something similar."

Alyssa held her coffee cup between both hands and rubbed the edges with her thumbs, thinking. "Does it even matter?"

James wiped his hands on a brown paper napkin, thinking. "It matters. You did a good job writing this. Now it's just a matter of presenting it to the directors of our department."

"It's just the facts." She took a sip of her coffee. "The attack wasn't malicious or planned."

"I know."

"Do you think Fox will let us present the report like this?"

James thought of his answer and how Fox was the first one to suggest the kid might be telling the truth. "I'm pretty sure he will."

He made the paper bag into a ball and threw it in the trash before standing up.

"Where are you going?"

James grabbed the papers and put them inside a crisp new manilla folder. "We're going to present this to Fox."

"Right now?" Alyssa shot out of her seat and ran her fingers over her short, red coils, perhaps trying to push them into place.

"The sooner we get his buy-in, the better."

Fox's office was located on the old side of the Clover Co. complex. The modern renovation of the other floors was supposed to get to Fox's side of the building soon, or so building management kept promising year after year. James worked under Fox for his whole career at Clover and had never once seen any improvements to that side of the building. They didn't add the windows they promised, and the carpet stayed the same sad sandy color for five years.

James put his best game face on and opened the door to the office.

"Good morning, Honey."

"James!" Fox's secretary smiled when greeting them. "I see most of the Delta Unit is here. To what do we owe this visit?"

"Is the Commander in? We've come to drop this off." He pointed at the papers he was holding.

Honey's smile wavered when she saw the folder. "You finished the report! That's great!"

James lowered the folder and exchanged a look with Alyssa.

"What's wrong?"

Honey gave him a slight shake of the head. "We received some news about the case."

"Did something happen?"

"It's not my place to say. Commander Fox can see you now."

Fox gave the papers a once over and set them down on his desk.

"I have good and bad news," he finally said, breaking the silence. "The good news is that we could have used this report and made a solid case in front of the Military Department Directors. Very nicely done, Alyssa."

"We could have?" Alyssa asked, and James felt her shift next to him.

"That's where the bad news comes in. We received this last night." He put a powder blue paper in front of them.

James' heart dropped as he read. This case had just gotten a lot bigger and a lot more complicated. "An escalation motion?"

"A what?" Alyssa asked next to James as he grabbed the paper and started reading.

"It's an order from the directors. We're to present the case in front of the company's Board of Trustees."

James put the blue paper back down on the commander's desk. "But why?"

"Someone thinks we are withholding information about the case and reported us to the board."

James felt the anger tense up at the back of his neck. "What are they trying to say?"

"That our Unit is trying to influence the directors' decision without presenting all the facts."

"Who would do that?" Alyssa said, indignant.

"The complaint was anonymous."

"Did they have any evidence? Why is the board taking this complaint seriously?"

"The board takes all complaints seriously, even if there's no proof. This will be an open hearing, which means the rest of the company will be able to attend." Fox shook his head. "It seems the directors thought the board would be better suited to give an impartial decision on the case."

Like hell they will, James thought, Robin's voice resonating in the back of his mind. The day he went to see her, she'd called it. The company wouldn't let this kid go so easily. They didn't care if he was malfunctioning. Someone was going to try to get him into their Unit. And their first step was to get the Delta Team out of the race, even if they weren't trying to get 0397 for themselves.

"What are our next steps, sir?" he asked, already feeling defeated.

"I'll try to push them back on putting this case out there for everyone to see. In the meantime, I need you two to prepare in case we have to present a report in a hearing." The commander turned to Alyssa. "Crimson, your code name is all over this report and the research logs. I cannot have anyone else present this case but you. If we do anything else, it will look like we have something to hide. Understood?"

Alyssa shifted in her seat next to him. "Yes, sir."

"Good. Tiger will help you prepare the presentation. I might not be able to make them drop it, and I have no idea what a hearing this big is going to look like. We'll have to make decisions on the fly." Fox picked up the report they had delivered. "I expect you to be ready to present this in twenty-four hours."

He put fourteen days of work and research back into her hands.

Getting out of Fox's office, James felt the greasy biscuit and sausage churn in his stomach. There was an extra weight on his shoulders, and when he looked over to Alyssa, he noticed she was feeling it, too.

Alyssa stopped walking on their way toward the group waiting at the elevators.

"What's wrong?"

"Why is this happening? We were supposed to just present the case to the directors so they could decide where to send 0397."

James sighed. "I thought the same thing. I talked to Robin about it and didn't want to believe what she said. They won't send him anywhere. Not to Hart Island and definitely not to Garden City."

"What do you mean they won't send him anywhere?"

"Keep your voice down," James warned. The people waiting for the elevator were discreetly turning toward them. "We need to be careful when we talk about the case now."

Alyssa looked at the end of the hall and noticed their audience, too She lowered her voice before continuing. "James, you saw what 0397 looked like during the interview. He needs help. How can they not send him to the Garden City Facility?"

"That's not the company's priority. This is only to see who gets to keep him."

Keep him. Like he's some piece of furniture. James felt dirty and regretted the words as soon as they left his mouth.

"Why hold a hearing, then? Why not just toss a coin?"

James shook his head. "Some sort of appearances must be kept up."

Alyssa looked up suddenly, her expression giving away that something was breaking inside her. "You have to present the case, James."

"What? I can't. You heard what the commander said. If we change leads now, it will look suspicious."

"What if Fox is also playing this game?"

"Fox isn't trying to keep 0397."

"How can you know that? You said it yourself: sending 0397 to the Garden City Facility isn't Clover's priority. Fox is part of the company, too If he's also trying to keep 0397... I can't be a part of that."

James looked into Alyssa's electric-blue eyes. There was a glint of mistrust he'd seen before. At some point in their Clover careers, every GENE figured Clover did not care for them. That program that had promised a better life, a stronger body, or a chance to become a hero lied to them. GENEs weren't safe, and they couldn't leave.

The muscles on his shoulders tightened up, and a restless fire burned inside him. "What if I told you there was a movement looking to protect rogues like 0397?"

Curiosity glistened in Alyssa's eyes.

"And what if I told you that movement had a mole inside the Military Department?"

Alyssa looked back at Fox's office. She understood what he wasn't saying, and curiosity transmuted into something stronger. It was a small but powerful spark, like the one trying to keep a fire alive during a harsh winter storm. "I'd want to join them."

Hot, orange liquid came out of him in another bout of vomiting. It splashed all over the white tiles. He heaved. He couldn't place the white tiles in front of him. They were dull and sanitized. They didn't catch the sick green gleam of the overhead lights.

With his ears ringing, he closed his eyes and tried hard to place himself. This wasn't the White Room. A smell of bleach hung in the air. There was someone else in the room with him, but he couldn't place them either. The vomiting sounds coming from the second person in the room made his mouth water again in disgust. He forced himself to ignore his nausea and focused instead on the memories that weighed heavy over him.

He'd held hands with two people at some point that night. There had been a live energy running between them and vibrating inside them. That energy pulsated along his spine and increased in intensity with every passing second. It crackled like electricity and exploded out of him.

Everything went dark after that. Screams flooded the room. He might have been screaming at some point, too

A whirlwind of memories and thoughts that didn't belong to

him trapped his mind. A connection had been established that night. Three minds linked together to share a common space of consciousness. He pictured three pools cascading knowledge into each other.

Miguel gasped for air and remembered who he was. Looking down at his shaking hands, he recognized them. He ran his hands over his body, owning it again as he separated his memories from the ones of two other people. The realization crawled from some dark corner of his mind.

Daiyu. Her real name is Daiyu. A smile spread across his face.

Miguel stood with a slight shake in his limbs. Even with all the new information in his mind, he still had so many questions. He looked around for Daiyu.

Three walls defined the length of the constricted room. The metallic barred door defined its purpose. This was a jail cell, and it was empty but for him and the blond guy in the navy jumpsuit.

Miguel found him still crouching over a puddle of his own puke just like he had been a moment ago. He tried to place the blond's name, but nothing came to mind. There was a connection between them now, but it was hard to trace it. The details about him were a tangled mess with big gaps of nothing in-between.

The blond tried to stand up, and he almost stumbled over as one of his legs failed him. Miguel moved to help him. When he touched him, an orange electrical spark flew between them.

The blond turned and growled at him like a hurt dog. He took a step back, fear written all over his face.

Miguel retrieved his hand. There were traces of the live energy from before still vibrating inside him. "You're afraid of electricity." The fact popped up in his pool of knowledge. "Sorry, I might still be charged."

The blond scoffed. "I'm not afraid. I just don't like it." He looked at Miguel sideways. "What the hell was that? What happened to the other room?" He looked around. "How did we get here?"

Miguel bit his thumb. The answers were somewhere in him, but he couldn't reach them. It was just as if they had been blinked into the cell.

"I'm not sure. I wanted to ask—"

"Daiyu." The blond completed his sentence for him. "That's the girl's name."

"Yes."

"How do we know that?" The blond paused and studied Miguel's face. "Or you. But I know your name. I know your life." He held the side of his head and winced. "How's that possible?"

"We need to get out of here and find Daiyu. Maybe she'll be able to explain everything." Miguel looked back at the heavy metal door. "Can we get out?"

The blond looked around and shook his head. "I've tried before." A bitter smile spread across his face. "This is my cell."

They looked for ways out of the cell for a couple of minutes. The only objects in the room were the metallic bed frame in a corner, the metal table, and the heavy lock on the door. In the end, Miguel and the blond sat in silence around the cell while contemplating solutions.

Miguel didn't have any ideas. "You know, we might just have to wait for her to make contact again."

"How do you know that?"

"I've always had to wait for her to come. I think she's like a battery. She might be recharging. Whatever she did back there must have taken a lot of energy..."

The blond gave him a noncommittal grunt as an answer.

Miguel tapped his fingers on the metal table. "So, what are we going to call you?"

"What do you mean?" the blond asked in a monotone voice from the spot he'd claimed on the bed.

"Well, we were in each other's heads and know a lot about one another now. But I still don't know your name. How come you don't remember it?"

"I'm not sure," he responded with a sigh as he sat up. "Why is a name so important? Seems like everybody wants to know it these days."

"You mean the people from the interview?"

The blond lifted his eyes to him, surprised by his knowledge of the interview. "You saw that too?"

"Only what you remember, but most of your memories about it are confusing." Miguel shrugged. "I couldn't see people's faces or get what they were saying most of the time. It's like they were speaking in a different language."

"That's because they were. I had to use this weird headset to understand them..." The blond furrowed his brow. "How are we even understanding each other right now?"

Miguel had to think about it. They clearly didn't speak the same language but could understand each other just fine in the shadow world. He racked his brain for information, hoping this would be one of those things he just suddenly knew.

"I don't know." Miguel shook his head. "Daiyu might be the only one able to explain it."

The blond acknowledged his answer with a grunt.

Miguel's attention went back to the room around him. "What kind of trouble are you in, anyway?"

"I don't want to talk about it."

"Fine." Miguel twiddled his thumbs. He clicked his tongue. The sound echoed in the room. "You still need a name, though."

"Agh. If it's so important, I guess you can call me this." He pointed to the name tag on his jumpsuit with the numbers 0397 printed on it. "Everyone else does," he said, rolling his eyes.

"That's dumb." Miguel twisted his face, disapproving. "I'm not calling you that. You need a real name."

"Yeah, but I don't remember it."

Miguel shook his head. "Well, that can be good! You get to choose your own name—at least until you remember."

"Really?"

"Uh, yeah! If it were me, I'd call myself something cool. Like Brix or Titus. You can have one of those if you want."

The blond shook his head and chuckled. "I think I'll pass. Those names don't feel like me."

"Don't you remember anything about your name?"

The blond closed his eyes, brow furrowed in concentration. "I think... someone said it was the name of an angel or something. I can't remember what it was or who said it."

"The name of an angel? I like that." Miguel thought about it for a second. "You know, *Ángel* is a good name from where I come from. People would say Angel here."

The blond looked at Miguel and gave him a smile that, for the first time since he'd seen him, didn't have a hint of sarcasm or aggressive undertones.

"I kind of like that."

"Yeah?"

"I think I'll keep that one, for now."

Miguel nodded, and a big smile spread over his face. He stood from his chair and extended his hand in front of him. "Hi, I'm Miguel."

"Angel."

They shook hands. Angel's metal hand reminded Miguel of the White Room and the panels mounted on its walls.

TIGER_

J ames scoffed and brought his mug to his lips. "What a load of crap," he whispered to himself. He was reading the front page of the *Gray Harbinger*'s December fifth issue.

In late November, an explosion in the Development District caused a district-wide electricity shortage. Almost three weeks later, the district is still in the dark. Authorities are still investigating the cause of the explosion, but all evidence points to three faulty generators and a possible clerical error. The Department of Power will be running a diagnostic of all the generators in the city in hopes of avoiding another explosive incident...

The bitter taste of coffee lingered at the back of his throat. Clover's PR Department had finalized their cover of the Blue Flamingo case's events. Anything that impacted any civilians got covered to protect the GENE secrecy. It happened all the time. They cooked up a story and paid witnesses for their silence whenever necessary. Someone at the Department of Power must have received an early Christmas bonus, courtesy of Mayor Wade and Clover's own Mister O.

A generator exploding had to be the laziest cover to explain damage left by an Electrochemical GENE. Then again, GENEs existed way before he joined the company, and he'd never heard of them or suspected their existence. Perhaps he didn't care enough, or maybe the signs weren't as obvious back then. GENE variations had gotten far more ambitious in the last decade. For now, it seemed that all that had to happen to protect them was put a lazy cover-up story in the news.

Was keeping them a secret really for their protection? Would he live to see GENE secrecy uncovered?

James took another sip of his coffee and drove his conflicting thoughts away. There were far more pressing issues that needed his attention. He looked at the clock on the far left of the cafeteria. He had to be at the Oval Room in thirty minutes.

A late call from Fox last night informed him their case had been approved by the board. The commander failed to convince the directors to keep the Blue Flamingo case in the Military Department. Now the Deltas had to present their case at a hearing in front of the Board of Trustees.

Correction: Alyssa had to present it. He sighed. If only he'd been the one to write that report three weeks ago.

I guess everyone must start somewhere.

James' thoughts swam back to the first and only time one of his cases turned into a board hearing: the case of Dave Maverick.

He'd never met Dave as Clover's Military Department was too big to meet most folks, even if they worked in the same branch. At that time, James and Robin had been the Delta Duo for a year and dealt with several cases. Nothing too big to make waves in the company, but less than a handful of their cases had been about dealing with rogue GENEs.

Dave Maverick had been in the Electrochemical program, probably one of the first ones to be made in the States. As his powers aged and he went through his mutations, something didn't sit well with his genetic code. While on a case in Boston, Dave had received GENE clearance to use his abilities, and they backfired. The electricity in his powers covered every inch of his body. Dave became a walking high voltage electrical charge and lost control of his mind. When the rest of his Unit tried to help him, he attacked them, thinking them enemies.

Robin and James had come in with a containment chamber for Dave. He found Dave cowering in a warehouse, desperately trying to turn himself off. James convinced him to walk into the chamber and promised he'd find a way to help him go back to normal.

In the end, the case grew so large that a board hearing was necessary. When the rest of the departments learned the details of the case, it divided the company. Most people believed Dave should be put in cryogenic sleep until the company could help him, but others were sure this would be a waste of resources, and it would be extremely difficult to fund. They said Dave Maverick was too far gone and should be submitted to the Exit Clause. In the chaos of the hearing, James wasn't able to present his point, so the board decided to dismiss the hearing and deliberate on their own.

For two years, he did his best to find out what had happened to Dave Maverick. He was only able to find out the board had ruled him salvageable and that he was currently in the Garden City Facility. Had the doctors figured out a way to turn him off? Or was he still asleep in the same chamber James had convinced him to climb into? He might never find out.

With a heavy heart, James stood up from his table and took his almost untouched breakfast. He hoped the same wouldn't happen to 0397, but he feared something worse awaited him.

By the time a whole sea of people finished getting inside the Oval Room, it was twenty minutes later than the originally scheduled time for the hearing. James' hopes of this hearing not getting as big as Dave Maverick's were crushed the instant he walked into that room. There had barely been any space for him to sit, and people were still coming in. Most of the new arrivals would have to stand at the edges of the room.

How did this case get so big? James thought as he examined the crowds. Cases that gave units like his big breaks at the company were usually hard, but he never expected this company-wide circus.

The Oval Room looked like a modern Roman Colosseum. The seats extended all around the room in rows that grew exponentially wider. The center of the room served as a stage. All the focus of the audience would be on the big holographic projector, the podium where the presenter stood, and the long table where the board members sat.

James looked down at the stage and found Alyssa and Fox near the podium. He remembered what it was like to be down there, Fox at his side telling him the audience was going to explode whenever he showed the apprehension of Maverick.

"Cryogenic chambers are expensive," Fox had told him. "But they are also the only way to keep an Electrochemical under control. People funding this technology will have something to say about it. Ignore the crowds; keep talking unless the board interferes."

If James didn't know any better, Fox was telling Alyssa something similar. He'd seen enough cases to know the crowd always had something to say. And it was hard to keep a cool head when standing at that podium with hundreds of people yelling over you.

James hoped that at least the board would interject and keep the crowd under control. He took a long look at the board's table. The board hadn't changed any members since the Dave Maverick case. He wondered how much help they would be to the Deltas this time around.

James saw Fox lead Alyssa to the board's table, probably to introduce her to all six members. He started with the board's chair, Genevieve Page. A woman with little time for flexibility, Page wore her head shaved, intense prints on her suits, and the coldest gaze James had ever seen. If the audience got out of hand, she'd be the one to set order in the room. Perhaps she'd decide to help the Deltas. Then again, when James met her at Maverick's hearing, the only thing she had to say to him was, "I trust you'll stay out of trouble, Adamant Tiger."

His face tightened.

Most of the board members received Alyssa with polite indifference. And then there was Mister O. The demeanor at the board's table changed when Mister O and Fox shook hands. The handshake lasted an instant, but its frigidity spoke much of the history between them. The tension reached James all the way to his seat in the eighth row.

"Hey, beefcake, you're gonna have to squeeze a little if I'm gonna sit here."

He turned to find Robin trying to claim the spot next to him. She wore semi-rimmed glasses, her long silver hair down and over one shoulder, and all of her usual overconfidence. She looked nothing like the sick woman he'd seen a couple of weeks ago. She was still a woman on disciplinary leave, however.

"Robin!"

"Yes, it's me. Hello. Now move so I can sit." James did as she asked and watched in awe as Robin took her seat next to him. "Thank you. These heels are fabulous but not at all comfortable." She had a copper four-leaf clover attached to the lapel of her teal blazer. It caught the light with a dull shine.

"What are you doing here? You're supposed to be out for at least another week."

"Eight more business days, according to that silly suspension slip."

"Does Fox know you're here?"

"Of course not, and he doesn't need to know. He has his hands full with this case." She looked at James and rolled her eyes at his blank expression, the purple of her eyes muted by the tint of her glasses. "Relax. I wouldn't be here if I knew the big Commander would mind."

James sighed and took one big hand to massage his temples where a migraine promised to settle in. The last thing he needed was someone complaining about Robin's presence when she wasn't supposed to come within a hundred feet of the Tactical Floor.

"So? What's the score?" She stretched her neck to scope the room better.

Now it was James' turn to roll his eyes. Hell would freeze over before Robin could take something seriously.

"We're in trouble. The board wants this hearing, and Fox is convinced this is just a front so someone can keep the kid in their Unit. He thinks we should stick to the facts and drive the Unit Recommendation."

"Shit. Then why aren't you down there? Didn't you write the recommendation?"

"No. Alyssa did."

Robin turned to him with a smirk on her face, "Attagirl. Who knew she had the guts?"

James scrubbed a hand over his mouth before answering, "Yeah, I guess it's a good thing."

Robin arched her eyebrows. "Uh oh. I expected sad James, but this is big-sad James. Lay it on me, big guy."

"Sorry, I just really wish it was me down there." James sank in his chair. "All of this is just too...familiar."

"I knew it. You're thinking about the Maverick case." Robin sighed. "You need to stop blaming yourself. It's not healthy."

"I told him he'd be fine, Robin. I promised him."

"I know." Robin patted his shoulder. "And now you need to personally save all the rogue GENEs out there."

James scoffed. "I don't know about that. All I know is that this case was going well until someone complained about us."

Robin stayed quiet for a second, perhaps mulling on what he'd just said. "What do we know about that complaint?"

"Nothing. Just that it was anonymous."

"The timing of that complaint is very interesting," Robin said as her eyes focused on something in the distance. James wondered if that gaze was set on someone specific or if she was zoning out.

"What do you mean?"

"Isn't it interesting that the end of the year is coming up? Every year, each department is asked to return any funding they didn't use in the year. Unless..."

"Unless?"

"Unless they have a groundbreaking discovery. Then that department gets more money and even a pat on the back. Wouldn't you consider the study of a new GENE variation to be groundbreaking?"

James felt sick and, for once, he was glad he had had no appetite for his breakfast. The lights flickered above them, like in a theater, announcing the hearing would start soon.

"Oh, mystery solved," Robin whispered with a forced smile on her face. She put her hand up as if to say hello to someone from far away.

James looked over and found Esteban Tomassetti in the

distance. Esteban spotted them and waved at them like they were longtime friends.

"I don't think we'll have to look far to figure out who submitted the complaint. Guess I'll have to miss Alyssa's big moment after all."

"What are you going to do?"

"I'll do some digging, see what I can find about this whole thing. Maybe we can get the upper hand for a change."

Robin stood up and exited the room.

James turned his focus back to the center of the room as he saw Alyssa climbing the podium. A sense of deja-vu struck him. He remembered himself on that podium, thinking how unfair everything seemed. A case that was so straightforward shouldn't have become this circus. There had been no justice for Dave Maverick, and he had a feeling they would find none for 0397.

The lights flickered a third and final time, and the room went silent. Showtime.

Alyssa's walk to the podium felt eternal. She could see in her peripheral vision the lights dimming for the audience. The chairwoman stood up to deliver a speech and kick off the hearing. None of her words registered with Alyssa.

When she climbed to the podium, she found her notes in front of her, along with a black clicker for the holographic projector. Like an amateur singer on opening night, Alyssa looked up, searching the audience and letting the silence in the room wash over her. Her mouth went dry.

With a snap of her clicker, a red Clover logo fired up in front of her and stayed suspended in midair.

"Thank you, Madam Chair." Alyssa's voice boomed on the speakers around the room. "Good morning, esteemed members of the board. Calling the case number JD-0397 under Unit Delta, code 77-84."

With another click, the Clover logo was replaced by a digital copy of the report. "On November 18 of the present year, a call entered Clover's emergency line at 1:57 am. The call came from the New Graysons' Police Department requesting backup for what looked like an Enhanced entity-related incident. Unit Delta was assigned to the case under Commander M. Fox. The team established contact with the suspect at 2:24 am; apprehension of Suspect 0397 was confirmed at 3:01 am."

The next slide revealed a picture of 0397. "This is Suspect 0397. He remains a John Doe as his identity is still inconclusive. The suspect had no translator chip, and the cross-reference against the Global Database using facial recognition came back negative."

She heard some murmurs in the back of the Oval Room. She imagined they were about how young the suspect was. Most Enhanced soldiers were younger than twenty-one years old. Clover personnel outside the Military Department were sometimes taken aback when they found out that most recruits started their Enhancements as early as eleven years old. She could have scoffed at the audience's surprise. Ever since The War, child soldiers were a fact of everyday life people chose to ignore.

Alyssa refocused on her presentation and braced for what was coming next. "After a medical assessment, Clover doctors and medical staff reported him to be, without a doubt, Enhanced." The next slide showed the audience the comparison between the DNA chains. "Samples taken from hair, blood, and saliva show that Suspect 0397's DNA shares some resemblance with Transhuman GENEs. But the similarities with other GENE classes stop there."

She clicked for the slide to change, and the audience exploded in a series of excited whispers. 3D models of 0397's silvery arm and leg shined in front of the audience. "These are 0397's mechanical parts. Clover's Medical Department determined they are pieces of biotechnology. They've theorized that all of 0397's Enhancements are meant to support the integration of said technology with his nervous system." The crowd's excitement grew, and she felt like she was leading the auction of a rare item. Alyssa ignored the anger growing in her gut. "Manufacturing of his Enhanced abilities, their origin, and their nature are still unknown."

She took a deep breath, trying to be discreet. If the audience was already going crazy with the little evidence she had shown them, they were sure going to go nuts with the videos.

"The Delta Unit worked with security videos from the club and nearby traffic lights to piece together a recall of the November 18 events."

With a final click, the video compilation played on the hologram. It showed a busy street on a typical Friday night in the Arts District. Soon, 0397 made an appearance. Despite having seen the same succession of events nearly a hundred times, her heart still stopped. She watched the red convertible stop next to 0397, the cup breaking against his body, his immobility as he watched the passengers of the convertible drive to the Blue Flamingo club. 0397 crossed the street without looking for traffic and walked right into the door of the club. What had it all been for? To demand a new jacket, money, an apology? Or had he really gone in there to kill them all?

The video transitioned to the inside of the Blue Flamingo. Images of fake fog and neon lights inundated the projector, and booming music filled the Oval Room. People gathering around the door and shouting followed by laughter and whooping made her think there had been a fight. Phone camera flashes flooded the scene, and even in the poor illumination and quality of the security videos, Alyssa saw the club's security detail intervene. Someone fired a taser, and 0397's screams flooded her senses. It was a shrill, bone-chilling sound of something breaking inside him. Alyssa witnessed the last part of the video sequence that made sense to her. After that, all she could piece together was chaos.

People screamed. Fear spread inside the club, and people trampled each other trying to make it to the emergency exits. Shots were fired. A security guard called people to stay calm and follow him to safety. Another called the cops on their radio. The hearing's audience held its breath in cold silence as the sounds of mayhem filled the Oval Room.

The video transitioned one last time to the outside of the Blue Flamingo. Somewhere in the madness of the moment, 0397 had walked outside the club, following three people who Alyssa recognized as the passengers of the red convertible. He stood on the sidewalk and stared at them as if they were nothing but targets. With the precision and timing of a machine, 0397 rose his metallic arm, and a cyan light shone in his hand. Three small objects flew from between his fingers with a movement that imitated a knife thrower's. 0397's plasma disks hit their targets on the back of their legs, a shot to immobilize them without killing them.

In the distance, a single police car blazed his way, sirens wailing. The plan of the police was obvious. They'd meant to speed up and run him over. The public in the Oval Room murmured.

Suspect 0397 stood motionless as if calculating the police car's distance and velocity. When the vehicle was about to hit him, he jumped in the air, backflipped, and landed behind the car. 0397 threw two disks at the vehicle's back tires. The cop car veered left and right, the driver trying to regain control. In the end, New Graysons' finest crashed against a nearby fire hydrant, and their hood lit on fire.

One of the policemen made it out of the car and pointed his gun at the suspect. He gave a warning shot that 0397 didn't heed. The cop fired three times, and 0397 avoided the first two shots. The last one grazed his side but did nothing to slow him down. 0397 reached the cop, snatched the gun away, and crushed it in a silvery fist. He smashed the cop's face on his knee and left him unconscious just as police reinforcements appeared in the distance.

Four officers climbed down from the armored car in full tactical gear and pointed assault rifles at 0397. He managed to take cover behind the crashed police car, waiting for an opening. Once he got it, he leaped a good five feet in the air and fired a new quartet of plasma disks that immobilized two of the officers. 0397 landed on the ground, and something like a shield emerged from his metallic forearm. He used it to get close enough to disarm the last two standing cops with military-grade maneuvers.

The audience in the Oval Room went nuts.

"Look at him go!" Someone gasped loudly from the back rows.

Alyssa turned her head, looking for the person responsible for the comment, but soon realized the whole room was participating in the commotion of surprised whispers and bewildered conversations. Her heart beat against her chest, and she forced herself to keep watching the video in spite of the audience.

More sirens came from the distance as 0397 finished disarming the last cop. He looked up and fled the scene, running towards a parking garage, away from ATM cameras and streetlights. And just like that, he had taken down the whole security staff at the club, six gun-blazing cops, and two police vehicles.

Alyssa waited for more cheers or even for the audience to clap, but the room fell silent once more. At least the people in the audience had the decency to recognize how inappropriate cheering would be. The spectacle they had come to see was over. She doubted any of them would listen to anything else she had to say.

The videos disappeared with another snap of her clicker, leaving instead the Clover logo floating in the middle of the room.

"Our Unit has concluded that the attack on the Blue Flamingo wasn't planned, but rather, it was a result of 0397's abilities malfunctioning with his brain chemistry. Research conducted by the Psychological Department showed damage to the suspect's temporal lobes and brainstem. Their hypothesis stipulates that this damage might have been present as a result of his Enhancements, and that it was exacerbated by the electrical charge club security utilized while trying to subdue the suspect. Our Unit recommends that he be placed into a rehabilitation program at the Garden City Facility. Our partners at the Psychological Department have also identified him as a candidate for memory recovery therapy and genetic cognition integration."

Alyssa's mouth went dry again as she concluded the case report. The time to present the facts was over. The real challenge was about to start. The board members would come at her with questions, and she better be ready to answer them, for the sake of her Unit and 0397.

"Thank you, Crimson," the chairwoman said. "The floor is open for questions. Members of the board, the floor is yours."

"Thank you, Madam Chair." Jim Rogers, the liaison of the American Military Department, was the first one to speak. "If there are no objections, I'd like to kick off the board's floor time. To me, it is very clear what we are seeing here. There were clear oversights while crafting this young man's abilities that make him vulnerable to lose control. Nothing that a rehabilitation program can't fix. Is there any information from the auxiliary departments that would go against the suspect going to the Garden City Facility, Crimson Thunder?"

Before Alyssa could answer this, the man with the Spanish

lisp in his voice spoke. "Excuse me, Head of Department Rogers, allow me to disagree. To me, this young man is a danger to the regular public. Look at all the destruction he has caused in such little time. He doesn't belong at the Garden City facility; he belongs with the Terminal Cases."

The air went out of her. She expected the board to mention Hart Island, but Mister O had come straight out and said it. Terminal Cases were Enhanced people that had no chance for redemption. Being declared Terminal earned you an express ticket to the Exit Clause. If the Board decided to side with Mister O, 0397 could be killed tomorrow.

People across the room gasped while others whispered in agreement. Head of Department Rogers cleared his throat and stood up, claiming the floor for himself, his microphone raising as he did from his seat.

"Thank you, Mister O, your feedback is always appreciated. But let's not jump ahead of ourselves, shall we? There are still several things to consider, not to mention that this is the time for questions, not deliberation."

Mister O snickered. "This is just like you to defend an individual that is clearly terminal."

"Assigning an Enhanced entity to Terminal Cases is an overly extreme solution," Rogers answered, his tone stern. "We should observe all the evidence before taking drastic measures."

The Chairwoman turned to her peers, regarding them with a calculating look. "I see your point, Mister O. Wasting a rehabilitation program on a dangerous GENE would impact our resources, especially because this GENE was not produced in-house. But I also understand we should proceed with caution, as Head of Department Rogers has pointed out. Mister Bigagli..." She turned to the Head of the Psychological Department. "This is more your territory. Is it too soon to make this move?"

"It isn't uncommon for GENEs to lose their grasp on their

executive functions. In these cases, they believe they are in danger and see the need to attack others, but most rogue GENE cases are reversible," Bigagli said. "The need to apply the Exit Clause should be our last resort."

"Shall we vote for this?" Rogers asked. "Although it looks like we are leaning towards reviewing the evidence."

Mister O glared at him briefly but smiled just as well. "Yes, perhaps it would be worth reviewing all evidence." He gave Alyssa a brief, dismissive glance. "I'd like to understand your team's experience when apprehending the suspect, Crimson Thunder. My department had to, after all, come up with two cover stories for a single mission."

Alyssa felt weak in the knees. If Mister O couldn't send 0397 directly to Terminal Cases, he would attempt to discredit them to rule out their recommendation. Every worst-case scenario kept coming true.

The tremor spread from under them, slow and with a hum. Before Miguel could make out what was happening, the room around him shook. The metal table and bed frame rattled like the wagons of a moving train. The trembling ended almost as soon as it had begun.

Miguel and Angel shared an inquisitive look.

"What was that?"

"An earthquake?" Miguel answered. He had never felt one in the shadow world before. "Weird."

The heavy metal door opened with a crank as if someone on the other side had opened a vault. Miguel stood up from his chair, expectation fluttering in his stomach. There it was. The signal he'd been waiting for from Daiyu.

"What do you think is on the other side?" Angel asked, doubt in his voice.

It looked to Miguel like Angel preferred staying in his cell to finding out what awaited them on the other side.

"I never know. The shadow world is like that." He shrugged. "There's only one way to find out."

Angel combed his hair back with a silvery hand, his face full of reservations.

It felt like an eternity ago, but Miguel remembered the doubt he used to have when he first started interacting with the shadow world. He wanted to know if things were real before engaging with them. Everything was a lot safer that way. Maybe it would have been easier for him to have someone to push him to take the first step. Maybe he could be that for someone else.

He walked to the door and pushed it open. He looked over his shoulder. "Are you coming?"

Angel sighed and nodded before standing up from the bed. He followed Miguel out of the cell.

Stepping outside the Clover Holding Facility made him feel like he'd been transported back into the actual world. Miguel never expected to walk back into the Main Clover Building's lobby. The crispness of the new place they had arrived to made it almost real. But the stillness they walked into was unnatural, and it confirmed this was still the shadow world.

The lobby was a place he encountered every day. He went through it while going from his living quarters to the Academy building or to his Enhancement appointments. He was too busy dodging people on his way to the elevators to notice how big it was. The lobby had the shape of a dome with glass panels for a ceiling. Natural light showered the whole lobby, making it look bigger than it already was.

Angel walked past him, his pace slowing down as he took the new place in. He looked up, and Miguel followed his gaze. Above them, a rare sunny day spread despite the harsh winter. The rich blue of the skies had an underlying cool color, like a watercolor painting going from blue hues to a grayscale palette. The gray light hurt their eyes.

Miguel looked back at Angel with his hard blue jumpsuit and the words *Clover Holding Facility* printed on the back. The question of what sort of trouble Angel was in floated around in his head. From their connection, Miguel knew he had good in him—he could feel it in his bones. His willingness to help them spoke to that. But then, how does a good person end up like him?

"Are you okay?" Miguel broke the silence.

Angel seemed to wake up from a trance. "Yeah..." He answered without looking at him as if wanting to enjoy the view for just one more second. "It's just been a while."

The quietness of his answer lingered with Miguel as he remembered his own time in a border detention center. That was in the harsh Mexican desert and not this cold city. The only view he got for a while had been the sad white walls surrounding him. It was even hard to tell the time of day.

Angel turned back to him and looked into his eyes, perhaps recalling Miguel's memories from their connection.

They stayed like that for an instant, sensing each other with a closeness Miguel had never felt before. It was like sharing his brain, his self, and his soul with another human being.

With the despondency of both their lives washing over them, Angel turned away, breaking the link. "What's this place, anyway?"

Miguel was grateful for the distraction. They both knew where they were from their connection, but a change in subject just might wash away sad memories. "This is the Clover Building's lobby."

"You said Daiyu could control the locations we landed on. Why would she send us here?"

Miguel's brain stretched to find an answer. When nothing came, he wished Daiyu was there to guide them. She had been his guide through the shadow world up until now. They were lost without her. "We need to find her."

"How did you find her before?"

"I didn't. She was always near. The doll was always there, too"

"You mean that strange one in the red dress? I saw it, too In my dreams, right before she'd appear."

"So, if we find the doll, we find Daiyu." Miguel paused, overwhelmed by the size of the Clover Building. Where would they start? He sighed. "I don't even know where—"

"Wait." Angel interrupted him, his voice low and sharp. "We're not alone."

Angel had his eyes set on something at the other end of the lobby, the part of the building that led to the Clover-issued living quarters. His indecisive demeanor was gone. A black cloud set over his eyes, and his expression grew harsh and centered.

In spite of his most basic instincts, Miguel looked in the direction of Angel's gaze. A shapeless shadow rushed in the distance, faster than his eyes could follow. Was it coming towards them or going away? A mix between a wet growl and a deep exhale sent a slow chill rolling down Miguel's spine. The sound was unlike anything he'd heard before. It spoke of something feral and predatory.

Miguel's heart went to his throat. Angel's hand instructed him to stay still. The lobby felt too open now, and the words *easy targets* quivered in the back of his mind. A second growl bounced around the empty lobby, growing fainter as it went deeper into the building.

And then, silence. Calm settled around them as if danger had left the building altogether.

"I think it's gone," Angel said. "At least now we know where not to go."

Miguel's hands trembled as he brushed the goosebumps away from his arms.

Angel said something else, but Miguel could not make out the words. Something went from wrong to worse when Daiyu linked with them. This place was not safe like it was when he'd traveled through with Daiyu, and he didn't know what awaited them. He didn't know what it meant for them or what it meant for Daiyu.

The ground beneath them shook. And this time, the tremor expanded fast, with a low rumble.

L eaving the stuffiness of the Oval Room before the
hearing ended was even harder than James antici-
pated. The ideal scenario apparently was to wait until
the spectators had left through the many exits, flowing streams
of sweaty men and women in business attire. But staying a
minute longer with his cell phone vibrating insistently in his
pocket was making it harder for James to hide the fact that he
had the mobile device he should've left at his locker. He cursed
himself for forgetting to leave it behind and apologized to the
people around him as he tried to exit the eighth row. James
endured the disapproving looks and comments and exited the
Oval Room in the middle of Alyssa's statement.

Even if he had been able to stay, James wasn't sure he had
wanted to listen to any more. Alyssa had accounted for the time
spent combing the area around City Hall, tracking and fighting
their suspect. She then faced some uncomfortable questions
about her decisions in battle. That gave Mister O even more
ammunition to highlight how much trouble it had been to cover
up the incident. He was making the whole Unit look beyond
incompetent.

James looked at both sides of the foyer, making sure he was alone before pulling his phone out of his pocket. He saw Robin's profile picture glow on the little screen before answering with a low voice.

"Finally. I was starting to wonder if you were ignoring my calls. What's happening out there?"

James grinned, noticing the slight tone of annoyance on his partner's voice over the line. "The hearing's still going. Can't exactly answer in there. I shouldn't even have my phone with me."

"What's taking them so long? I expected you to be done already."

"They're grilling Alyssa about how we handled the field mission. It's not pretty."

Silence on the other side of the line told him Robin didn't like what she was hearing. "I guess it shouldn't be surprising. They'll try to discredit our Unit so the recommendation is ruled invalid."

James knew she was right. How seriously could the board take a recommendation from a group of rookies? "Yeah. And get this: O has been pushing terminal cases since Alyssa finished her statement."

Robin let out a sarcastic laugh. "Of course he is. That explains some things, I guess."

"Did you find something?"

"I did. Suppose someone had an alternative motive to complain about us for any reason. What would be the point? You'd think spite wouldn't be worth the effort. Profit is a better angle. Did you know the company can still make money out of GENEs that go into the Garden City Facility?"

A dark feeling settled in his chest. "No, I didn't."

"Well, they can. They collect data from Enhanced peoples in rehab to aid in the Enhancement Process. Think of it as going back to the drawing board and figuring out what went wrong. This, of course, takes a long time. At Garden City, they at least try to prioritize the well-being of their patients over their research."

James caught on to what Robin wasn't saying, and he hoped against hope that he was misunderstanding. "Hart Island doesn't have that limitation. It's a research center."

"Correct." He heard the click of a keyboard from the other side of the line. "Apparently, someone thought there would be a way to edge research forward faster. In the last couple of years, there has been an increase of terminal cases in Garden City. Which means an increase in transfers to Hart Island."

"No...," he breathed.

His head spun. GENEs malfunctioned every day because of new trends in Enhancements. Not everyone was cut out to mutate successfully, and Garden City was there to give extra help to those that couldn't. James thought about how fast new Enhancements and new GENE types were developing. He always assumed some new breakthrough in tech was making that happen.

How naïve. He could have kicked himself.

"James, even if we win this hearing, we lose." Robin's voice continued in his ear. "0397 will end up in Hart Island no matter what."

Robin was right. James thought of all the people Special Response Units had ever sent to Garden City. He thought of the ones his own Unit had sent there. And now 0397 could just turn out to be another one of them.

"How is this happening?"

"I have no idea. I've tried to look into the transfer requests and the Garden City database, but I just don't have the credentials to gain access."

"Shit. We need to talk to Fox, then."

"I'll leave that to you."

James heard a soft thud in the foyer that jolted him out of his conversation with Robin. He lifted his eyes and looked behind him. The door to the Oval Room was closing, but the foyer was empty. He felt watched nonetheless.

"I have to go." James rushed his words and hung up on his partner.

"Tiger!"

James jumped at the call of his code name. Esteban Tomassetti was walking towards him from the elevators, which were in the opposite direction of the Oval Room. James didn't see him leave past him. Had he just used his powers in the Clover Building?

"Don't tell me you just hung up on that call because of me." Esteban swayed towards him, an overconfident skip in his step.

James pocketed his phone as if that would make Esteban go away. The underlying aggression in James' tight-lipped smile was impossible to hide.

"Didn't expect to find you out here by yourself, Tiger. Especially with your newest addition getting torn to pieces in there."

"Funny." James gritted his teeth. "I didn't expect to see you out here either."

"Oh, I just had to stretch for a little while. This hearing's running long."

The urge to punch the leader of the Beta Unit rose inside of him. They wouldn't even be having a hearing if it wasn't for Esteban. James took a deep breath and reminded himself what was important. Besides, even if he threw a punch, he'd never connect. Esteban would dodge that faster than James could blink. His code wasn't the Blazing Cheetah for nothing.

"Who was that on the phone?" A smug smirk spread over Esteban's face.

"Komodo felt sick and had to excuse herself from the hearing. Just wanted to check on her."

"Right. It sounded more like you had her check into some information."

Fire built up in James' chest. All the stress of the last few weeks weighing him down, the case exploding in their faces, the information he'd just received from Robin, and now getting caught on the phone by Esteban. It was too much to take all at once. If he could not fight Esteban, he would not play politics with him.

The words came out of him with the strength of a sledgehammer breaking a wall. "Cut the crap. What do you want, Esteban?"

The younger man stopped cold, surprised at James' harshness. He seemed to recover quickly. A smirk spread across his face like fire licking away at a piece of wood. He let out a sort of laugh that reminded James of the yelp of a hyena.

"I'm glad you find this entertaining." James crossed his arms over his chest, staring Esteban down.

"This is why I like you. Direct and to the point." He shook his head and pointed at James with his finger in a lazy movement. "Very well. I'll get to the point."

Esteban lifted his eyes. The smile was still on his face, but not in his golden eyes. "Your Unit is in dire need of direction here. I'm sorry to say, you guys bit off more than you could chew with this case. There's a file at your desk right now. It'll point you in the right direction."

James scoffed. He expected anything to come out of Esteban's mouth. Anything except that. "We know you sent a complaint about us to the board, and now you want me to believe you'll help us?"

"You can believe whatever you want." Esteban's smirks and lazy demeanor were gone. "But you've been in this business long enough to know that this company owns us, and most of the time, we do things because they are direct orders." A dark shadow covered his eyes. "And just sometimes, we get to do things so other people can't sleep at night."

Behind Esteban's eyes, James saw such unspoken hate that his resolution to not trust him faltered. "Which one are you doing now?"

Esteban clicked his tongue as if trying to decide if he should keep talking to him or not. "One of my teammates died, and you know what that sick fuck O had to say about it? He told me to find a replacement as soon as Medical confirmed the disposal of her body. He denied my request to notify her family."

A sharp pain stung James' chest. No words reached his mouth.

Esteban Tomassetti laughed a bitter laugh. "I'll let you decide which angle I'm taking." He turned to walk away and gave him a last look. "That file will stay on your desk until the end of this hearing. Only an idiot would pass the opportunity to make a copy of it."

The whole Clover Building shook with an intense hum. The glass ceiling rattled. Miguel ran to the edges of the lobby, following Angel to find cover. When the tremor peaked, he fell to the icy marble floor. He clenched his eyes shut.

The trembling stopped. In the aftermath of it all, the lobby returned to its original stillness.

Miguel held onto a fountain for support. The koi fish inside swam away like nothing had ever happened. A closer look at the fish revealed they swam in a pattern that looped on itself. As he got up, he noticed the water inside the fountain, the clouds in the sky, and everything else around him moving in patterns. It reminded him of an old video game. He didn't spot that before.

"Miguel?" Angel's voice drifted in as he approached. He put a hand on his shoulder and gave him a once-over with a furrowed brow. "Are you hurt?"

A warm smile spread across Miguel's face. "I'm okay." No one had looked after him like that since he arrived in the United States. Most doctors and researchers cared for him but not about him. "You?"

"Yeah." Angel looked around with a watchful eye. "What do you think that was?"

Before Miguel could answer, the sound of a long exhale and a wet growl rolled into the lobby. Miguel's breath caught in his chest. The shapeless shadow from before was back. Had the tremor called its attention? Miguel didn't want to stay another minute to find out.

Angel's sharp gaze came back. His voice was stern and quiet. "We should keep moving."

The only place Miguel could think of going next was the Medical Wing. It was the farthest place from the living quarters and the shapeless shadow they saw in the lobby. He led Angel through the waiting rooms, the labs, and even through the Recovery Hall. There was no sign of Daiyu or her doll. Uneasiness weighed heavy at the back of his neck. They were no closer to finding Daiyu than when they first left the Clover Holding Facility.

Empty corridors echoed with their steps, and Miguel's mind swam in unanswered questions. The psychic connection Daiyu had formed between herself, Miguel, and Angel came and went in waves. Sometimes, he could sense Angel's presence or his feelings. He could visualize details from his memories as if borrowing pages from the book that was his past. Other times, Angel's essence hid away from him, like it was trapped behind a vault.

He had tried to control this newfound psychic ability, had tried to use it to feel Daiyu's presence and find her. So far, it hadn't worked.

Miguel rubbed at the tension in his neck. From their connection to Daiyu, he knew something was wrong. Looking at the shadow world now only confirmed it: the tremors, things moving in a loop, and that creepy shadow roaming near the living quarters' building. A troubled chill perched on his limbs.

"Where to now?" Angel asked from behind him.

They had come to the end of the Recovery Hall. With the elevators in front of them, they could either explore the Hippocratic Hall one floor up or try to explore lower levels.

"I guess up one floor."

"Let's go, then." Angel motioned to move, but when Miguel didn't follow, he turned to him. "What's wrong?"

Worry stirred in Miguel's gut. "What if we don't find her there?"

Angel pursed his lips. "Then we try the rest of the building, I guess. There's not much we can do, right?"

He felt Angel's essence and understood there was an underlying concern in him he'd been trying to hide.

"You feel it too, right?" Miguel's voice came out small and defeated. "Something bad is happening to Daiyu. And she's getting worse."

Angel lowered his eyes. "Yeah. You said the tremors didn't happen before. And I'm guessing that...thing back there wasn't around before either."

"It wasn't."

Silence fell upon them. Their anxious thoughts merged. Did Daiyu have a time limit over her head?

"What if we split up?" Miguel blurted out, even though the idea felt incomplete in his brain. "We get to cover more ground like that."

"We're not doing that." The look Angel gave him made him feel like a little kid.

Miguel furrowed his brow. "And why not?"

"Are you serious? That shadow thing is still out there. Something could happen to you."

"Just me? What about you?"

"I can protect myself." Angel made a fist with his metal hand and knocked on his metal leg to illustrate his point. "Can you?"

He knew Angel was right. Miguel didn't have any powers to protect himself. He still rolled his eyes. "Fine. Then we need to leave this part of the building, go somewhere else. We've been looking in the Medical Wing for hours for nothing."

"How can you know it's been hours?"

"It feels like hours. This place is huge! And how is that important right now?"

Angel put his hands up, trying to make peace.

Miguel took a deep breath and shook his head. "Let's just keep looking in the Medical wing. We can figure out what to do next if we don't find her."

Once in the Hippocratic Hall, Miguel stood in front of Doctor Johannes' office. He tried to think how many times he'd visited this place since he arrived at Clover. He'd lost count. That door was always open when he needed to see the doctor. But when he reached for that door's padlock in the shadow world, the door didn't budge.

"So? Can you open it?" Angel asked from behind him.

"No." He sighed. "I don't get it. The shadow world reflects places we have visited before. I've been in this office so many times. How come it won't open for me?"

Angel scratched his forehead. "Could you just get into this office as you liked before?"

"Well, no. I need an appointment."

"Then that must be it." Angel shrugged. "You can't enter

this office in the real world without an appointment, just like I can't walk out of my cell. It's the same here."

Miguel frowned, thinking. The shadow world was a realm filled with weird things. Jellyfish, falling spores, and now shapeless shadows. But things still happened in a logical order. Gravity was the same. He could still feel cold and pain, or even get hurt. He couldn't fly or go through walls. If a door was closed to him in reality, it would still be closed in Daiyu's dreamlike shadow world. "What do we do?"

Angel grinned. "We make do." He moved past Miguel and went to the door's padlock. He cocked his head and made a claw with his silvery hand. In a clear-cut move, he drove his fingers into the padlock and clawed it out of the wall in a tangled mess of wires.

Miguel gasped and let out a laugh. "Dude!" Without its mechanical lock, the door inched open. "You gotta teach me how to do that."

Angel smirked and slid the door open.

Just like every other place they had visited in the Clover Building, Doctor Johannes' office felt sterile, untouched. It felt like no one had been in there, like the entire place had been just pushed out of a fresh and neat package. The only evidence tying the workroom to its actual world copy was the music in the background. The tones in the lyric-less music were strange, but Miguel couldn't figure out why.

He pushed his doubts away and forced himself to focus on why they were there, and Daiyu wasn't there. "Let's look for that doll."

"If it isn't here, we should go to all the offices on the floor. Maybe one of these doctors knows something about Daiyu."

They separated and started looking for the doll inside of the medicine cabinet, on and under the desk, and even in the coffee station. Miguel's heart dropped. There weren't many places where they could look. It was just a tiny office.

"What's with that music?" Angel asked.

Miguel got up from where he was searching under the desk and looked at him. Angel was right. Every other place in the building had been still. Quiet.

"Doctor Johannes always has the same music in his office."

"How'd you know that?"

"He's my doctor. I see him every other Wednesday." Miguel almost jumped up and down as the revelation took form in his mind. "I must have listened to the songs he plays a dozen times. It's always the same."

"But something's different here? In this world?"

"Yes! I've never listened to this song before! It's new to me."

"If you don't know it, and I don't know, it must come from Daiyu's memory! She has to be close to this place then or...or maybe the doctor sees her, too?"

"Yeah!"

"How can we check?"

"Well, everything's here." Miguel pointed to the computer at the desk and at the filing cabinets lining the walls. "Doctors keep records of their patients, so we can look for her name in the files."

Angel gasped out a laugh, charged with relief and hope. "You get the computer, I'll get the cabinets."

"I've got something!" Miguel said, triumphant.

After what felt like hours of digging through the files in Doctor J's office, Miguel ended up finding a patient record at the very bottom of the list. Zhihou D. An old picture of Daiyu displayed next to her name.

The information in Daiyu's file confirmed some of Miguel's suspicions. Clover didn't give Daiyu her Enhancements. The company somehow got their hands on her afterward. When he opened the file, he found it to be almost empty. It contained basic information about Daiyu like her weight, her height, her age, and the color of her eyes. White.

According to the document, her GENE class was under investigation. Doctor Johannes had left a note that was like a suggestion of what to call Daiyu's genetic variation: *Synaptic* was written in cursive with a stylus. Miguel scrolled down and found nothing else. The rest of the file was empty but for a file number and the word *Confidential*.

"How's it going over there?" Angel asked from the other side of the room.

"I don't have a lot. There's her last name and some basic details about her. There's also a number here."

"What number? All these folders have numbers on them."

"It's ZDS15-34."

Angel looked around in the filing cabinets. He went from one to the other and soon pulled out a thick manilla folder with multicolored page markers sticking out from all around it. "Got it!"

Miguel jumped out of his seat by the computer and hurried over. The beaten-down folder was in such bad shape. To Miguel, it looked like these records had been passed between many doctors. They must have read and reread its contents day after day.

Angel opened the file and glanced over the stack of documents. He looked at Miguel, a mix of anxiety and excitement on his face. "There's a lot to dig through."

"Let's split it up."

They read and read about Daiyu, finding out more about her than what they already knew from their psychic connection.

Daiyu was a Genetically Enhanced Entity made by a different company. Her variation was rare. There were only two more people like her in the world. The description of her abilities was inconclusive. The research team at Clover could not figure out what she was supposed to do. They understood that Daiyu's ability enhanced the communication between her neurons and that the chemistry of her brain was different. Her response time to stimuli was so fast that it looked like she could predict what would happen.

"I don't get it. Does this mean she can see the future?" Miguel asked.

"Let me see." Angel read the passage from Doctor Johannes' notes. He had to read it several times to understand what the notes were referencing. "I can't really understand it either; there are a lot of medical words I don't know. The doctor thinks her brain can see patterns in stimuli and predict what will happen, so it sounds kind of like she can predict the future."

"Wow, how does her brain do that?"

Angel shrugged. "I don't understand how this works." He pointed with his human hand to his metallic one. "I just know it does."

Miguel could no longer hold his curiosity. "What is it?" He couldn't figure it out, not even through their connection.

"My arm?"

"Yeah."

Angel looked at his arm for a while. He flexed his fingers and watched how the alloy caught the light. "A weapon."

They shared an awkward silence.

"Uh—You're Enhanced, right?" Angel asked, a note of curiosity in his voice.

"I will be." Miguel smiled. "The doctors say I'll be going through mutations soon. I don't understand all of it, but I guess it means I'll get my powers soon."

"That's crazy. I don't think I ever knew there were other people out there with powers."

"There's a lot of them, and Clover makes a bunch of them."

"What for?"

"They say we're made to protect the world, to make it better."

Angel stayed quiet, perhaps contemplating the answer. "We should keep looking into Daiyu's folder."

"Right."

They returned to reading in silence for a while.

"Listen to this," Angel said. "'Subject continues to show signs of mutation while on life support. The department has moved her to Unit 34 in intensive care to continue monitoring her progress.' The date is October 15—they moved her to an intensive care unit two months ago."

"Maybe that's where she's at!" Miguel burst into smiles. "The hospital wing is close. It's one floor above us. I bet intensive care is upstairs, too."

Angel looked at the file, then at him. "Why would she have to be in intensive care?"

Miguel felt his smile wash off his face almost as fast as it had arrived. *Intensive care* had an awful ring to it.

"Maybe we should find out?"

They sat reading the rest of Doctor Johannes' notes. Many of the notes made no sense to Miguel—the words were long and complicated and spoke of chemicals and care routines.

From what he gathered, Doctor J was Daiyu's most recent doctor. The Clover Medical Department had passed her around for a year because no one knew how to help her. Doctor J was her last hope.

"What does 'prognosis' mean?" Miguel asked while reading more on the current state of the patient.

Angel looked up from his manilla folder. "I think it means what will happen to someone who is sick. Why?"

Miguel handed him the file and waited for him to read, hoping he'd be able to decode that message.

The quiet of Angel's voice delivered a painful blow to his gut. "She's dying."

Sunlight gleamed in rivulets through the window. The waters of the marina made the midday sun dance inside the waterfront Rogers' penthouse. Robin took a look outside at the oddly sunny day. This would probably be the last sunny day they'd get before the real winter hit New Graysons. There were just a few days left in the year, and Robin wondered if by the first quarter of the new year, she'd still have a job in the Special Response Units. She hoped her visit to the penthouse would solve all of that.

She heard the soft heels of Allison Rogers as she joined Robin in the sunroom. The mature woman was garbed in a silk wrap dress designed in pale rose colors that fit her skin tone to perfection. She had a drink in her hand that was almost empty of its orange liquid.

"Darling, I hope you don't mind, I've gotten us a couple of mimosas to chat while we wait for Jim."

A tall butler followed her with a silver tray containing two tall glasses. Allison sat in front of her at her lavish plush chair. The butler sat the drinks in front of them and disappeared so smoothly that Robin forgot about him almost instantly.

"You'll have one with me, won't you, dear Robin?" Allison asked. "Jim hates it when I drink alone, but if he came home to find us drinking together–" She took a long swig to finish her first drink. "Well, that's a different matter."

Robin gave Allison a complicit smile and took a sip of her drink. It had far more champagne than what she would have expected from a regular mimosa. Robin decided she'd nurse her drink for as long as she could. She never minded drinks at lunchtime, especially when it came to Allison, but if she wanted to talk shop with Jim Rogers, she'd better do it with a clear head.

"So tell me, dear," Allison prompted, seemingly content with their drink arrangements. "What brings you to us in the middle of the week? We were expecting you and Richard for brunch next weekend."

Robin smiled. Her relationship with the Rogers extended beyond Clover. Senator Richard Night, her adoptive father, knew Jim Rogers from college. Since she was a child, she'd attended Sunday brunches once a month to chit chat. "I've actually come to talk business with Jim."

Allison smiled, a mischievous spark lighted in her eyes. The way the sunlight hit her face at that moment made her look even better kept than she was. "Is it a professional favor that you need?"

Jim Rogers was the head of the Military Department in the US. He'd always said that if she ever needed a favor in Clover, she needed only to ask. She was always politely said she'd think about it—she knew this was a one-time offer. It wasn't like Jim could solve all her career problems for her. If she was ever going to cash in that favor, there was no better situation than the one she and the Delta Unit were in right now.

"Something like that. I'd never ask if it wasn't important."

"I see. You don't need to give me any explanations. A woman should look for her career above everything else." She swirled her drink. "I was a career woman before I married Jim and could have stayed like that, I just liked the poison too much." She winked and finished her second drink with a swig.

Robin just smiled at her, but she wondered if the story of how she became such a trophy wife was a little more complicated.

"I see you two are having fun." Jim Rogers said from the doorway. "Nicolas told me you were in here."

"Darling! Welcome home." She stood up on a swirl of silken skirts and planted a kiss on Jim's cheek. "Robin came for a visit, isn't she a doll?"

"She is. Robin, how do you do?" He went to her and gave her a hug.

Robin smiled and put her best face on, preparing to ask Jim to slip back into his work self in his own home. Was that guilt she was feeling?

Surely not, Robin rarely felt anything at all, and she was not about to start feeling guilty. It was shame, she realized, as Jim invited her to sit back down and turned to ask Allison to get him some refreshments. What a shameful situation it was to have to come to one of the department heads in order to get out of a situation her Unit shouldn't be in.

"Robin, I heard you were out of commission for a few weeks. How are you feeling?"

"Oh, that?" Robin waved a pleasantly dismissive hand in front of him. "Just an occupational hazard. The doctors at Clover made me feel better in no time."

"Good, good. I'm glad. We don't want to lose one of our star GENEs."

Robin smiled in spite of herself. The talent she possessed was often referred to by Jim and the Senator as untapped and not being used to its full potential. They kept telling her that her abilities would be good enough then to get her to wherever she wanted to be at. Her career just needed to bloom first.

"So Robin, what do we owe this wonderful visit to?" Jim said while he unbuttoned the cuffs of the white dress shirt under his blazer. "I wasn't expecting you until next week."

"Well, Jim," she smiled her most winning smile. "I'm sorry to say this isn't a mere social call. I'm afraid I have a favor to ask."

Jim chuckled, "Don't ever be afraid to ask a favor from me. You know I appreciate you and your Unit. How can I assist?"

Robin swallowed, thinking his tune might change after she was done talking.

"You know the kind of situation my Unit is in right now."

"I'm surprised you know about it. Are you not on leave?"

"I always like to keep an eye on my Unit whenever possible."

"How diligent." He sat back on his chair, a pleasant look on his face. "Please, go on."

"In fact, I've been doing my own research on the case of the Blue Flamingo."

Jim seemed to be taken aback by this. He gave her a serious look, the kind a father might give their child when they talk of going off to Europe to see friends they've never met instead of going back to college. Robin resented the look but swallowed her pride nonetheless.

"What do you mean?"

"I've been looking into the report and talking to some outside sources my Unit was not able to contact while they worked on this assignment."

"And all of this while you were on leave?" Jim continued with the same grave look on his face. "You wouldn't be trying to influence my vote on this matter, would you?"

"Absolutely not. I just have a theory about what's

happening behind the scenes, and I need your knowledge to prove it. Particularly regarding the Exit Clause. I need to know the ins and outs of it."

"Such an unsavory topic, dear. Why do you want to know more about this?" Jim considered the topic for a moment. In the end, he gave her a blank expression. "I'm not sure I like this, Robin. I must say this is a risky situation for you."

"I know how it looks, Jim, believe me. But once you hear what I have to say, I'm sure you will agree this conversation was a necessity."

Robin let her request to have a conversation about the Exit Clause sink in before she continued.

"Jim, I have a bad feeling about this case and this hearing. I have a feeling that even if the board votes in our favor, we might still see 0397 making a trip to Hart Island. It is just a matter of time."

Jim Rogers looked at her with a flash of understanding coming right off his gaze. "Very well. Tell me more."

"I've found some records indicating that someone in the board has a contact in Garden City who has, in the past, transferred subjects to Hart Island. All that was required was a signature, no questions asked."

Jim Rogers put a hand up, stopping her from saying more. "Do you have a name?"

"I do."

"Please, Robin. If you know what's good for your career, keep that name to yourself." He sighed. "I understand what you are saying, and let me tell you, you are dealing with fire here."

"I know."

"Why are you doing this? Are you intent on saving this kid's life?"

Robin stopped for a second and understood she had no intention of saving anyone's life. But James did.

"Jim, I've been on the sidelines far too long. You've always said I play the game with a lot of care and warned me that I'd have to pick a side one day if I ever wanted to succeed. I really think this is it. This is how I choose a side. It's sink or swim."

Jim sighed. "And you had to go and choose Millard Fox's side? Very well." He took a deep breath. "Listen, there is a third option here. A third outcome for this case and this 0397."

"Which is exactly why I came to you."

Jim lifted a finger. "If I help you, if I help you get to this option, I cannot be associated with the Delta Team anymore. There are rumors about your commander's involvement with the Enhanced People's Rights Movement. The company doesn't like it, so I shouldn't either." His eyes grew serious, calculating. "When you leave my home today, we no longer know each other, and your team will lose my support. Any aid I have given the Delta Unit, anytime I've overlooked this Unit's shortcomings, all of that is over."

Robin thought about it for a second. This was exactly what she had expected from Jim. She knew that if she went to him for help, they might risk losing his protection. She knew the Deltas might have been disbanded many times before if it wasn't for him, but this could also help them rise above their station. They would never move up, and otherwise, Mister O would only make scapegoats out of them, and then Jim Rogers would not be able to help them. They risked more staying with him, she firmly believed that.

"I understand."

Allison's heels came back from the parlor into the sunroom. They took this as a sign that their conversation was over, and Robin had made her choice.

Allison came carrying Jim's lunch in a tray. Robin didn't look at the woman that had just joined them. "My, my, it got awfully tense in here. This must be some favor you've asked, dear."

"Not at all," Jim said. "This is just a new era in our Robin's career, isn't that right?"

"That's right." Robin raised her glass to meet Jim's. She smiled, thinking she made the right decision. She might have lost her biggest benefactor in the company with a single conversation, but she would now make her own way into a career. No more staying stagnant for her or the rest of the Deltas. This was going to set things in motion.

T he floor beneath them shook with unprecedented intensity. Miguel had no time to process Angel's words. Daiyu was dying.

He lost his footing and fell to the ground. The lights in the room flickered, and in the distance, a strenuous sound boomed. Was that a boat's horn?

"This one's gonna be big!" Angel yelled over the Hippocratic Hall's creaks and rumbles.

A wave entered Miguel's consciousness. He felt Angel's essence and the thunder of his heartbeat.

Angel grabbed him by his shoulders amid the darkness and confusion. "We need to get under the desk, come on."

They took shelter under Doctor J's desk as the office around them fell to pieces from the falling filing cabinets and the ceiling's plaster. Miguel closed his eyes, thinking his insides would liquefy from the shaking.

It took a moment for him to realize the quake had ended.

The fallout of the quake was worse than before. When he opened his eyes, Miguel found the world to be a gray mess. Fine concrete dust floated around them, and there was an eerie stillness in the air. Something else was off. There was a sense of uneasiness behind that stillness, like he'd entered a room he wasn't allowed to be in.

Coughing the fine concrete dust out of his lungs, Miguel crawled out from under the desk. Through the fallen ceiling, snow fell in. A biting cold filtered in.

"What the hell is going on?" Angel asked, looking out the office window.

Miguel ran to the other end of the office, bumping his friend's shoulder at the window. A shoreline painted the landscape outside. With a trembling hand, he pushed the window open. A warm breeze seasoned with seaside drifted in. Below the gray Clover Building, a shore town extended for miles under a sky painted with watercolors.

"Is that—" Angel's voice drifted in.

"It's San Gerónimo," Miguel whispered in response.

"Isn't that where you're from?"

"Yeah... My past is filtering through." His stomach lurched. "Yours is too, look." Miguel pointed at the snow falling through the hole in the ceiling.

Angel stood under the hole in the ceiling. He stared at the snow and extended his human hand to catch it. The snowflakes melted when touching his skin. He rubbed the moisture away. "What does this mean?"

Miguel shook his head. "It must mean Daiyu is getting worse."

Miguel walked to the window and rested his hand on the glass. The seashore town extended before the sea. A sunny day showered the cobblestone streets, meandering down to the shore. Colorful homes piled over each other, showcasing different levels of salt-stained rooftops. Miguel's breath slowed as he drank it all in. His eyes prickled with tears. San Gerónimo looked peaceful.

"Hey, so..." Angel took a step closer to him. "Most of your memories about San Gerónimo were happy. But at some point, everything got confusing. Dangerous. I couldn't understand what I was seeing."

"Me neither." Miguel breathed.

A darkness filled his heart. He never understood what had happened the last time he'd been in San Gerónimo. At one point, his whole life revolved around school, playing soccer in the evenings with his friends, and fretting over math and history tests. Change came in small bouts. A curfew was instituted, and no one would leave their homes after sundown. His family stopped listening to the news. School closed down. His neighbors disappeared.

"My dad said they came for the oil rig. They stayed for our fish."

"The Russians? What were they even doing out there?"

In the watercolor masterpiece that was the San Gerónimo of his past, he spotted a black dot on the horizon. It was a splotch of black ink, looming over a tiny town of fishermen and winemakers. The rig had been an empty steel structure since before he was born, a leftover from The War.

When the Russian militia came, no one asked why. They had guns while the townsfolk only had fishing nets and a predisposition to mind their own business. Miguel didn't know what the Russians had been doing in that rig. He hadn't suspected what they were doing when they invaded his town and settled in their compound. He couldn't understand until the man with the fire hands rolled into town.

Memories of the town square going up in flames played in his head. People screamed and ran from the militia. He stared at the man that destroyed his town with the touch of his hands. He remembered thinking how fast the flames consumed everything.

Miguel heard his voice speak the words, but didn't recognize it as his own. "They were making GENEs."

A jolt of electricity traveled through his spine, driving away his thoughts of San Gerónimo. The energy touched him with gentle strokes, like the tide from the sunny memory outside the window. Miguel closed his eyes and explored the energy. It was Daiyu reaching out to him. His mind filled with knowledge, and then she was gone.

Miguel took a deep breath and forced his focus to return.

"Did you feel that too?" Angel asked.

"Yeah." Miguel turned, a wave of worry washing over him as he finished processing the fresh information. "Daiyu is losing her grasp between realities. We need to find her. Soon."

Angel looked around the destroyed office and scoffed. "Things just keep getting better, don't they?"

"What is it?"

"Look at that." He pointed at the office's entrance. A piece of debris had fallen over, blocking the door. "We're trapped."

"Can't you just move it?" Miguel asked with a shrug.

Angel inspected the immense chunk of concrete with metal rods sticking out. He shook his head. "I'm not that strong."

"There has to be another door. Doctor J's lab is on the back of his office, and there's an emergency exit back there. Maybe we can get to Critical Care through there."

"Then let's go before the building shakes again."

Miguel gave San Gerónimo a last look before he led Angel to the back of the office. Behind the doctor's desk, someone had tagged a flush door with a plaque that read *Laboratory*. He'd crossed that threshold so many times that he pushed it open with the confidence of routine. An unnatural cold hit him from the room inside and stopped him dry in his tracks.

The lab reminded Miguel of the last time he'd woken up in the shadow world, back at his apartment. It looked as if the entire room was frozen in time. A sick green light shone over the laboratory, and spores floated around, suspended in the air. Miguel's skin crawled with goosebumps. Was it the cold? Or was it the harsh dread in his gut?

A wet growl followed by a deep sigh came from deep in the lab. A shapeless shadow stretched across the back wall. It was an enormous mass of tenebrosity, darker than ink.

"*Mierda...*" he whispered.

The inky shadow screeched at the sound of his voice. Its sound made his heart shiver, and it dove towards them like a bird of prey.

Miguel reacted just in time to close the door.

"I didn't think it had followed us." Angel's face paled. "Was it that big before?"

"It was not!" Miguel's heart hammered in his chest.

Snarls and growls came from the other side of the door. Miguel jumped away from the door, holding his breath.

"It wants a piece of us." Angel made his way to the other side of the office, toward the chunk of concrete. "Help me try to move this."

"But I thought you said..."

"Do you have a better idea?"

Miguel went to help. They pushed on the piece of ceiling as hard as they could. It did not budge.

Something like an explosion burst from behind the lab's door. Miguel watched with bulging eyes, unable to blink away the image of the door breaking. The door to the lab cracked as porcelain. The shapeless shadow crossed over through the cracks. Its unnatural growls and grunts filled the room.

Angel stepped in front of him.

"What are you doing?" Miguel's voice came out small and trembling.

"I'll fight that thing," Angel said simply as the black mass continued to sweep into the room. "When the coast is clear, go through the lab and find Daiyu."

"Are you crazy?! How are you even going to fight that thing?"

Angel shrugged. "I can at least distract it. Wait until it's safe, then find Daiyu."

Miguel's stomach went to knots. "I'm not leaving you here." How could he think this was a good idea?

"You sensed it too, right? Daiyu doesn't have a lot of time."

"But–"

"I can defend myself. Remember?" He showed his silvery hand, his eyes stern. "Go find her, I'll catch up."

The dark shadow growled in their direction. It swirled like a wind trapped inside a snow globe.

Angel cracked his neck and slid into a fighting stance. "Man, this thing's ugly."

The shadow screeched again and rushed towards Angel. It swirled around itself as it flew towards its target, narrowing into the shape of a needle. When it was close enough, Angel threw a punch, but it just went through the shadow. It was like punching the air.

The inky shadow enveloped Angel's arm with a loud, long exhale. It twisted around him like a constrictor snake wrapping onto prey. Angel twisted in its grasp, trying to break free. The shadow went into him, making his body jolt and paralyzed him.

"Angel!" Miguel cried out, the boom of his heart trashing in his ears.

Darkness traveled down Angel's body all the way to the ground. It stretched over the floor as if it were his own shadow. Looking at it twice revealed the shape of a man in a military visor cap. He held a cane in his hand. A neon-red eye shined through the darkness of the shadow.

Angel's terror boarded Miguel like a high tide. It became a

harsh, icy ball in his chest. The shadow creature had trapped his friend in its grasp, his consciousness ambushed in a whirlwind of sensations and unclear memories. Miguel's eyes darted from Angel to the broken door. The coast was clear for him to go.

Miguel gulped. He knew Daiyu didn't have much time, but how could he leave? He thought about what the Rangers of Earth would do. They would use their superpowers and fight the monster. They would save the day. Fear rose from the back of his spine and enveloped his mind and his soul. Miguel wasn't like them. Heroes had the strength to protect themselves or help others. He was just some kid.

With a sharp breath and his teeth grinding, Miguel forced the fear down. He might not have superpowers, but that didn't mean he shouldn't try to help. With his hands still trembling, he made his way to the shadow creature.

The dark creature had solidified while wrapping around Angel's paralyzed body. Miguel's brain stretched for solutions. Angel was running out of time. With the grim shadow twisting around his neck like that, he'd suffocate.

Miguel braced himself and did the only thing he could think of. He held tight onto the dark shadow and pulled down with all his weight. Touching it felt like touching a live, pulsating muscle. It brought thoughts of a boa constrictor to his mind. The dark shadow was hot to the touch, and it grew more scorching with every passing second. Miguel pushed through the pain and hung onto the black serpent's body with all his weight. Its grip on Angel eased.

The dark shadow growled. Cold sweat dripped from Miguel's forehead. The inky serpent's body pulsated, and its body grew hotter than Miguel could withstand. He let go of the creature, his hands shaking in pain. His skin was red and scorched black from touching the serpent. Without letting go of

Angel, the serpent growled again as it engorged, doubling its size.

Then, from the spot he'd been holding onto, a second black serpent grew. Miguel let out a yelp and jumped back. The serpent's second head lurched forwards and attacked Miguel. It wrapped around his waist and lifted him in the air like a rag doll. The shadow slammed him against the ground. Miguel grunted in pain. He fought to break free of the serpent's weight. The dark shadow lifted him up again, and the world spun in front of his eyes. The second time the shadow slammed him against the office's floor, Miguel's hearing went out with a boom.

He closed his eyes, darkness engulfing him.

Behind the darkness of his eyelids, Miguel saw an orange flare.

Something clicked inside him. A live force awoke within him. It jolted him awake and drove all the pain away from him. He heard the energy crackle from within him, wild and young.

Adrenaline rushing inside him, Miguel drove the energy out of him. Orange flares flew around the room, stinging at the shadow. A high-pitched scream came from it as it growled and panted. Its grasp eased on its prey, and its two heads backed away.

Miguel jumped to his feet, looking for Angel. He found him on the ground, coughing as he tried to recover his breath. Black marks stained his skin everywhere the shadow had touched him.

Miguel helped him sit upright. "Are you okay?"

"I'm fine." With a swift and precise movement, Angel threw something out of his hand. The disk flew past Miguel and landed onto the shadow serpent behind him. "Thank you for staying."

A smile spread on Miguel's face as Angel got up from the floor. "Did you see? I think I got my powers!"

Another bout of screeching came from the other side of the

office. Angel's weapon had gotten stuck on it. Earlier, Miguel's orange energy had driven it away. They could hurt it.

"Let's get them," Angel said, standing next to Miguel.

The two-headed shadow slithered towards them, letting out a battle cry of wet snarls. Miguel and Angel charged against it. Angel received the dark shadow with a kick. He made a fist with his metal hand, and a blade came out of his forearm.

Miguel let out something between a gasp and a laugh. "Oh, cool!"

Angel snickered. "Pay attention to yours!"

"Right." Miguel turned to the snake head coming his way.

He connected a punch with a hand covered by orange light. The shadow lurched back, screaming in pain. A wide grin ran across his face.

Miguel focused on the flares flowing out of him. He closed his hands into fists, focusing all his power on his hands. The energy filled him as he thought of how much he'd been waiting for this. All the doctor's visits. All the radiation and the hard recovery sessions. Everything he had endured during the past year had led to this moment.

Like swimming against the tide, Miguel pushed the energy out of him. He put one hand in front of him, aiming for one of the snake's heads. Orange lights beamed across the room.

"Shit, man!" He heard Angel exclaim as he backed away and out of the way.

Miguel lifted his other hand in front of him, letting another stream of orange light escape him. His attack hit both targets like sunlight scorching shadows away.

The shadow gave a woman's shriek that filled the room as Miguel's orange flares drove the shadow away. Miguel watched, amazed as the orange light filled the shadow like a balloon. The electronics in the office exploded. The papers on the ground swirled around as gusts of wind blew all around him. Miguel filled the dark shadow with energy until his vision blurred, and his ears rang.

Just as he fell to one knee with his head spinning, he saw the dark shadow swell up and burst. It exploded into smaller shadows that dissolved into the light. A long and quiet exhale was all that was left from the dark shadow in the room.

Miguel laughed, relief washing over him. He panted, and laid down on the ground, exhausted.

Angel loomed over him. "Feeling okay?" His reservations to touch him palpable all over his voice.

Miguel laughed. "I'm not charged anymore."

"Good." Angel offered him a hand and helped him sit up.

"That was awesome!" Miguel said.

Angel gave him a tired smile. "I've never fought anything like it."

"I've never fought anything before."

Angel gave a slight laugh and shook his head. "Let's go find Daiyu."

CRIMSON_

T he Delta Tactical Room appeared in front of her in a
blaze of rage. She could barely recount how she'd
made it out of the Oval Room and back into the
Deltas' office. She made her way back to her desk and stared at
it, a hot ball of rage stirred in her gut.

How dare they? She thought.

Many papers with frantic notes were scattered around. The
piles of reports from the Psychological Department adorned the
corners of the desk, and the electronic books evidenced her
work. She worked night after night trying to understand the
psychological reports, trying to determine if 0397 was dangerous, and how to present all the facts in her report. She spent the
night before the hearing looking for case studies that could help
her defend him. She'd watched the interview and the security
videos over and over again, trying to figure out what she would
say to the board.

She didn't admit it to herself then, but now she knew. She'd
been hopeful and far too optimistic, thinking the board could
truly care about what she had to say. She sat down, losing
strength on her legs.

The board members had not laughed in her face, but if they'd done that, it would have at least been honest. The way Mister O twisted her words and continually alluded to her novice status killed any argument she was trying to make in 0397's favor. He'd mentioned this had been her first time on the field and questioned Commander Fox's sanity to give her GENE clearance. After all, the destruction her powers had caused to the city's Industrial Sector was the hardest incident his department had to cover all year, and 0397 had endangered the public and the GENE secrecy with the aid of the Delta Unit.

By the time he was done talking, they'd run out of time. The first half of the hearing was over. Within fifteen minutes of his long-winded speech, Mister O had single-handedly wrecked her credibility and all her hard work. She had never felt more like a child.

Hot tears welled in her eyes. A raw life force awoke inside her, and when she closed her eyes, she could visualize deep-red lights over the dark backdrop of her mind. Alyssa took a deep breath, swallowing her tears, her anger, and controlling the electric life stirring within her. The last thing she needed was an electric explosion in the middle of her tactical office.

Alyssa looked around the empty office and remembered when Fox had first transferred her from the Records Room. Before apprehending 0397 three weeks ago, the only thing on her mind was to fly under the radar. She'd hoped to get a commanding recommendation that would send her home. That felt like a lifetime ago. It was incredible how much this case had changed her. She wondered if this case had changed the rest of her Unit as much as it had her. Would the verdict from the board affect them as much as she knew it would affect her? She pushed her feelings aside before her anger and frustration could rise and threaten to show up as electric energy again. She forced herself to focus on what she could control right now, and nothing else.

Alyssa looked at the digital clock above the door and realized if she didn't leave then, she would be late to Fox's office.

Alyssa sighed and rubbed at the tension at the nape of her neck. Maybe things were not quite as bad as she thought. She had a tendency to worry too much about things she couldn't control. Alyssa grabbed her jacket, and her last bit of hope for this case to turn better.

The meeting in Fox's office apparently started without her. Upon entering the office, Alyssa found Fox, James, and Robin all huddled around the commander's desk. They were looking at some papers and pictures. It took her a moment to realize it was her report and other documentation. Was that the Clover Military Handbook?

She must have opened that thing once after her transfer when she wanted to find out just how permanent her disciplinary leave was. The legal jargon danced around the issue so much that she ended up closing it, no closer to her answer. The rules for Enhanced Entities were never clear.

"Thank you for joining us, Crimson." Fox greeted her. "I thought you could use a break after the hearing. Komodo here brought us some interesting information on the case."

At least she wasn't in trouble with her commander. She was afraid that maybe she had forgotten the time of the actual meeting. Alyssa approached the table and saw several pictures of people she'd never seen before.

"Before we start," Fox told her. "I need you to promise me

that the information Komodo has brought to us won't leave this office. Ever. There is a lot at stake here, and I won't have our Unit jeopardized for this new information."

Pressure grew in her chest. "I promise."

"Excellent. Let me catch you up, then." Robin said. "In short, Mister O is behind the complaint to the directors."

"He is?"

"Esteban Tomassetti pretty much confirmed it," James answered. "I had my own run-in with him outside the Oval Room while the hearing was still going."

"Turns out he has people inside the Garden City Facility who are willing to send GENEs to Hart Island for him. The only thing he needs is to sign some papers. This got us thinking that even if we succeeded in sending 0397 to the Garden City Facility, we might actually lose him, too"

Alyssa felt an emptiness in her stomach. She hadn't felt such a despairing emptiness since she was told she wouldn't participate in the graduation ceremony with the rest of her UK team. If O had such power, then all the work she and James had put into this case was truly useless. Then there was really nothing they could do for 0397, and all her fears were a reality. She had really brought him back to Clover just to die.

"Alyssa? Did you hear what I said?" Robin's question brought her back to reality.

"I'm sorry... what was that?" Alyssa asked, feeling stupid.

"I said that fortunately, there seems to be a loophole in this whole thing."

Butterflies fluttered in her chest as if she had just gone downhill on a rollercoaster, and it was climbing up again.

"I went to Jim Rogers to investigate this whole Exit Clause business and how it works. Basically, there is a condition under this clause that says that Clover-owned GENEs are specially protected against the clause. The company has to exhaust all the other options before applying this clause to all of their malfunctioning and dangerous GENEs."

"I don't see how that applies to 0397," Alyssa said. "He's not Clover owned."

"But he can be," Robin said, a glint of victory shining in her eyes' purple haze. "All he has to do is sign a contract under Commander Fox. He'd be relinquishing his freedom and ownership of his powers to him and, thus, to the company."

"So, he basically becomes Clover property?" Alyssa wondered in the back of her mind if this was really okay, and then she remembered she, too was Clover property. She, too had signed a contract stating that her abilities were the company's. She'd been too young to know what that meant.

"That's right," Fox said. "We won't be getting him scotch free, but we'd at least buy him protection, more time to prove he isn't a danger, and that he can be an asset for the company in ways other than research."

Alyssa took it all in. She looked around the room at the people talking about the case and realized then that each and every one of them was Enhanced. They were all Clover property, even Commander Fox. She felt dizzy.

"Why is this his only option?" Alyssa asked no one in particular.

Fox straightened and looked at her with warmth. "I've been asking myself the same question for years. GENEs are not like other military contractors. There are no laws that protect us from what the company decides to do for us because the government is not supposed to know about us. No one is."

"But what can we do about that? It doesn't feel right."

"We start like this. Enhanced rights are all about making a stance, and this is the best opportunity to do it."

Alyssa considered his words and agreed that the board would never do anything about giving them rights. This really was the only way.

"Where do we start?"

The place they entered was nothing like what Miguel would have expected. He'd expected a hospital room, with Daiyu hooked up to a bunch of machines.

Instead, they found a lavish garden that belonged in a fantasy book. Miguel had seen nothing like it. Green, well-kept grounds extended for miles under a gray sky. It looked as if they had just showered in a perfect mid-spring rain, the ground squishing under Miguel's feet, soaking his red sneakers like walking on a full sponge. Lavish ponds and fountains spread across the gardens.

Six polished stone statues adorned them. All the statues were archangels, which Miguel recognized because of the golden wings and swords. Soldiers of the heavens, his mother called them. A closer look at the sculptures' faces revealed a likeness to Daiyu, Angel, and himself. Miguel cocked his head, taken aback. He searched the other three, but their faces were incomplete. It was as if the sculptors had only chiseled half of their faces.

Ahead, he found a girl in a traditional black silk dress—Daiyu. She had taken her shoes off and was standing inside a fountain. Her black hair draped over her shoulder in a braid. The loose strands of hair no longer floated around her like wisps of shadows. The mystical glow that surrounded her before was gone. This time around, Daiyu looked just like herself and no longer like the apparition Miguel had named Shadow Braid.

"Daiyu!" His voice rang fresh in the garden as if it were the first sound ever heard in that place.

Daiyu lifted one hand to say hello to them. She was holding a fisherman's net and something inside it. As they walked over to her, Miguel saw it held jellyfish as white as polished bones.

"You found me." Daiyu's doll smile curled on a tired face.

She held him in a brief embrace, her movements mechanical and awkward. Relief washed over them all. Miguel sensed her emotions as much as Angel's.

When Daiyu released him, Miguel saw that up close, she looked so tired. Her eyes had no shine to them, her iris a dull white. Black stains under her eyes revealed her sickness and frailness far more than before.

"What are you doing here?" Angel asked as Daiyu embraced him like they were lifelong friends. "Where is here?"

Daiyu looked around them and shrugged. "I'm not sure where this is. I've been hiding from the shadow, so I have to jump from one place to another. This is the latest location I've found." She looked at Angel with her head cocked. "I think this place belongs to you."

Angel looked around and shook his head. "I don't recognize it."

"You will." Daiyu reassured him. "The mind fixes itself; it just takes time."

"Is that what's happening to you?" Miguel asked, not able to hold his questions in any longer.

"Something like that." Daiyu went back to her jellyfish. She picked the net up and threw the jellyfish out of the fountain.

Miguel then realized that she'd been cleaning the fountain of dead jellyfish.

"My powers..." her voice trailed off as if she didn't want to say it out loud. "They're killing me."

"How?" Angel asked, his voice filled with worry.

"When I was back home, the doctors put me in a coma to awaken my first mutation." Daiyu grabbed the fisherman's net again and dipped it into the water. "They meant to wake me up when I was ready, but then they came for me."

"Who?"

Daiyu's silence lasted a heartbeat and her voice delivered the facts dry of all emotion. "Clover. They stole me away."

Miguel felt like someone had punched him in the gut. Clover was not like the people he'd read about in his comic books. Deep down, behind the promise of safety, he'd known that from the beginning. There was no ignoring it now.

"So this entire world, did you build it? Like in your mind?" Angel asked.

"In a sense," Daiyu's voice had the quality of a patient physics professor. "Our minds use dreams to sort through complex emotions and aid our memory retention. Being in a coma for so long created a need for my brain to place my consciousness somewhere, so it created this world." She shrugged. "Or at least that's my theory."

Miguel and Angel stared at her, trying to follow the explanation. Daiyu was only a few years older than Miguel, but she seemed so much older when she spoke.

"But the world you see around us, this shadow world as Miguel dubbed it, is not only my construct anymore." She lectured on. "This world is also made of places that exist in your memories, because your minds are now part of it, too"

"Is that why we can talk to each other?" Angel asked, his curiosity about this still fresh.

"Ah, that's right. Talking with others must have been hard in the real world." Daiyu offered him a gentle smile as if she suddenly remembered a painful detail about him. "Well here our minds are linked, so the need to speak to each other is inexistent."

Angel scratched the side of his head, mussing. "Does that mean we are not really speaking right now?"

"That's right. We're communicating on a psychic level, but our minds process the interaction as speaking."

Miguel's head hurt when trying to understand what Daiyu had just said. A different question popped inside his head. "If you've been in a coma all this time, how come you were able to visit us in our dreams?"

"I have not been able to understand that part. My mind is expanding, so maybe my powers are a lot stronger now."

"But even if they are stronger, they're hurting you," Angel said.

Daiyu nodded. "My body isn't ready to withstand this mutation for this long. I have been in this coma for months, when I was supposed to be in it for only a few weeks."

"So you needed space to expand," Miguel said, catching onto what Daiyu was saying.

"Correct. Before I reached out for help, my mind was ruined, overloaded."

"Which is why you couldn't just ask for help."

Daiyu nodded. "I needed to rebuild my mind. When you two agreed to connect with me in the White Room, we were linked and I was able to use you as a battery to fuel my efforts, and as external drives to host my abilities."

"This is incredible." Angel sounded half intrigued and half amazed, and Miguel had to side with him. How was it possible for Daiyu to connect with them on a psychic level and construct a world like the one she had?

Daiyu's muted excitement fell off her face. "But now, even with your help, my body won't be able to contain this mutation. If the doctors don't force me to wake up, my mind will eat itself."

Miguel's stomach went cold. They were right. The signs of the world crumbling around them and glitching them into different places meant Daiyu was dying.

"Okay, how do we help?"

"I need someone to go back to the real world and convince the doctors to wake me up. I can open a portal to send you both back, and that might be the last thing I will do." She stretched her hands in apprehension.

Angel turned to him, sadness written all over his face. "All of this will be on you. I'm... in a lot of trouble in the real world. I won't be of any use to any of you inside that cell."

Miguel glanced at Daiyu. For an instant, he saw an emotion he knew far too well. Fear and uncertainty of what the future held. The increasing suspicion that there would be no future. Something ignited inside his chest. Clover wasn't the all-good entity he'd believed them to be. The abilities they would give them might be tainted by all the wrong choices they'd taken to get there. Maybe superheroes weren't real.

But that didn't mean he couldn't act like a hero.

"I've got this. I'll go to Doctor Johannes and convince him to wake Daiyu up. He'll listen. He has to."

"I'll open a portal and probably disappear after that. After you jump inside the portal, you should wake up at the last place you were in the real world." Daiyu painted that perfect doll's smile on her face again and almost whispered. "Thank you. I might just make it thanks to you two."

She offered each a last hug, the only way she could repay them for their help.

Daiyu offered them a slight grin and turned away from

them. With a snap of her fingers, she opened a gap in the gardens. The rich green colors of grass and the gray of the skies swirled around that gap like oil colors mixing. The portal filled with a light so bright that Miguel and Angel had to shield their eyes from it. Frosty air blew around them, making Miguel's skin crawl and sending a shiver down his spine.

When Miguel opened his eyes again, Daiyu was gone. They were alone in those lavish gardens, the portal shining, waiting.

"I guess this is it," Angel said without looking at him, the cold air driving his matted hair away from his face. "I thought helping Daiyu would make me feel better about what the people at Clover say I did. As if it would somehow erase what happened if I helped her." He turned to him again, his eyes tired and dull like an old man's. "I know it won't, but thank you for helping me do some good."

Miguel smiled at him. It filled him with sadness at the thought of not having either Daiyu or Angel close to him in the real world. He was going back to being alone.

"Once I help Daiyu, I'll find you. Maybe we can help you, too"

Angel let out a dry chuckle and extended his right hand. "Something tells me I'll need all the help I can get. Thank you."

Miguel shook Angel's cold metal hand. "See you on the other side."

The light of the portal enveloped them, and warm energy lulled him back to reality.

Miguel opened his eyes, sweat-thick sheets sticking to his body and the taste of sandpaper in his mouth. He sat up on the bed, his limbs creaking like the baseboards of an old house.

The light of a winter morning shone cool blue through the

window walls. His Clover living quarters stayed just like he had left them. A half-eaten bowl of cereal and his tablet were still on his nightstand. His tablet blinked, warning him it was almost out of battery. He took it to check the time. Worry lingered on the back of his mind without him knowing why. He'd been gone for twelve hours.

Miguel shivered with a gasp as images of his journey in the shadow world hit him.

Thank you. I might just make it because of you two. Daiyu's words replayed for him.

Something tells me I'll need all the help I can get. Thank you. Angel said as they shared in a handshake.

How could all the things he lived with Daiyu and Angel fit in only twelve hours in the real world? With his heart and mind full of shared struggles and fears, Miguel's eyes filled with tears. When he stepped into the real world, he'd lost them. The uncertainty of recovering them weighed heavy over his shoulders.

A sudden realization jolted him out of bed. He was back in the real world to make sure that what Daiyu said were not her last words ever. His mission was far from over.

Soulful blues received him when he stepped outside the elevator and into the Hippocratic Hall. Doctor Johannes was in his office. Miguel made his way across the hall, the saxophone notes injecting him full of purpose. There was almost a mystic aftertaste to each note, a quality that brought Miguel back to that unreal place he had just woken up from. He stood outside of that office door, listening to the music filter through.

It was the song he heard in the shadow world.

Miguel took a deep breath and knocked. He half expected to find the shapeless shadow on the other side of the door.

The volume of the music died out. He heard rummaging inside the office and steps closer to the door. Miguel gulped, hoping he was in the real world and that nothing would jump out at him, especially not one of those shadows.

Doctor Johannes opened the door, "Miguel! We don't have an appointment, do we?" The doctor's tone betrayed his organization skills.

"No, we don't." Color rose to his cheeks. "I just need to talk to you."

The doctor must have seen the desperation in his eyes and didn't send him away. "Sure. Please come in."

Miguel followed him inside. The office looked just like when the last tremor hit in the shadow world. There were papers everywhere, open cabinets, and manilla folders piled on either side of the office. If Miguel didn't know any better, he'd say the doctor was in the middle of reorganizing his entire filing system.

"I'm sorry for the mess here." The doctor apologized as he cleared a chair free of manilla folders. "I know this place looks a lot better for our visits; Thursdays are research days, and I get carried away." The Doctor lowered the volume of his stereo. "Please, have a seat."

Miguel did so.

"So tell me, what brings you here. Are you okay?"

"I am." His heart pounded with uneasiness. "I wanted to tell you something about another one of your patients. Zhihou Daiyu?" The doctor's eyes flashed with a spark of curiosity. Miguel continued before he could ask anything. "Um, I know this will sound... crazy. Will you just listen until I'm done?"

The doctor gave him a warm smile. "Okay, I'll listen."

Miguel spoke of the first time Daiyu contacted him, and how his last visit hadn't been about borrowing more comic books. He confessed he'd been afraid to tell him about the dreams he'd been having. Miguel told the doctor about the last twelve hours he'd spent in the shadow world and about his journey to find Daiyu and understand what she needed help with.

"When we found her," he continued. "Daiyu told us you needed to wake her up. Her powers are eating her brain away, and there is no way she'll survive if you don't get her out of her coma." Miguel took a deep breath as if he had just finished a much needed glass filled with cold, fresh water.

For a moment, the only sound between them was the blues in the background. The doctor's eyes betrayed his judgment about what Miguel had just said. Miguel couldn't blame him. He had barged in on him and fed him a story that sounded to come straight from a comic book. Pure fantasy. Had he made a mistake coming to him?

"Doctor J, you have to believe me." Miguel's voice dropped to a whisper. "Please."

The doctor then took a deep breath himself, still looking worried.

"Miguel, what have you just told me is... incredible. I'll be honest with you because you just were extremely honest with me." Doctor J intertwined his fingers as he rested his hands over the polished desk. "My first instinct is to write off everything you told me and get you a medical order for a psych evaluation."

Miguel's heart dropped, threatening to break in disappointment. A sliver of hope hung on what the doctor might say next. "But?"

"But, you know things about this patient, Daiyu. You couldn't know this even if you hacked into my computer and looked through the files in this office. The information you just gave me is confidential. The scientist in me wants to explain how in the world you know all this. In all honesty, we don't understand how Daiyu's powers work at all. From what we do know, everything you're saying is possible."

"Does that mean you'll help?"

The doctor smiled. Jazz filled the silence between them.

"Yes, Miguel. It means I'll help."

The light hoodie he had on did nothing to protect him from the cold in the intensive care unit. When Miguel followed Doctor Johannes inside the small room, Miguel understood where all the cold was coming from. The cryogenic chamber stood against a wall, hooked to multiple machines. Aside from the whirring of the cooling fans and the soft beep that monitored Daiyu's pulse, the room was void of sounds.

Miguel approached the chamber to take a better look. The chamber looked like a spaceship's emergency pod, large enough to hold an adult's body. It reminded him of an enormous black egg, made of a smooth material that didn't reflect the light. It was as if the chamber could absorb all the light. The logo printed close to the bottom of the pod did not escape him. A symbol of a DNA chain next to a red star was the only confirmation Miguel needed: The pod didn't belong to Clover.

The clicks of a keyboard called his attention as Doctor Johannes set out to work. "Let's see how our patient is doing today. I'm glad you came when you did, Miguel. I was due for a visit up here, anyway."

With a final click from the keyboard, the egg released air like exhaust. A window opened on the face of the egg, large enough to see the person inside. Miguel's heart skipped a beat when he saw Daiyu. She was submerged in ice and blue light. Her hair rested in a long braid over her shoulder, and loose strands floated around her as the cooling fans kept the chamber going. Her blue lips and expressionless face made her seem like a ghost. She held a porcelain doll under her arm. Its bright red dress wrinkled under her grip.

Worry prickled Miguel in his side. This was the Daiyu he didn't want to find in the real world. She shared more qualities with the ghostly Shadow Braid than with the girl from the gardens.

"Interesting." Doctor Johannes' voice had a spiked tone of curiosity.

He appeared to be analyzing Daiyu's vitals on a series of monitors. He walked from one to another as if comparing the information on both. Doctor Johannes lifted the cover of a box attached to the wall that was a communicator.

"Front desk, this is Doctor Johannes Kingstone. Please tell Doctor Jessica Sharp to meet me in Unit 34 in intensive care. Tell her it's a code orange."

The doctor didn't wait for a response and returned to work at the monitors. Miguel had never seen him like that. It was like he was on a trance, looking at the screens in front of him and typing faster than he could understand.

Uneasiness settled on Miguel's chest, shortening his breath. "Is something wrong?"

"Miguel," Doctor Johannes' voice was firm and a little strained. "I need you to tell me what you remember about Daiyu's abilities."

"What?"

"We know nothing about how her abilities were engineered, and right now, we need to use all the help we can get. Tell me what you remember from the dream world you described before, or anything Daiyu might have told you herself. How do her powers work?"

Miguel's brain rummaged through his memories of the shadow world for information. "Well... I remembered reading about her abilities in the shadow world. It said that the connection between her neurons work like they can talk to each other faster."

"How could we have missed it before?" He consulted his monitors for a second. "What were the scientists in her research facility doing when they put her in this chamber?"

"Uh, she said they were inducing her coma, to help her mutate, and that we needed to wake her up from it."

Doctor Johannes stopped his frantic work as if Miguel's words had trapped him in an epiphany.

The door of the critical care unit opened with a beep. Doctor Sharp entered the room, followed by a nurse. "Doctor." She looked at Miguel with a furrowed brow. "Mister De Santos? What—?"

"Doctor Sharp, I need your eyes on these vitals."

Doctor Sharp gave Miguel a last questioning look and walked over to the monitors.

"Do you see her heart rate? It appears normal, but if we look at her brain activity over here," he clicked more keys. "You can see it declines."

Doctor Sharp fell in the same trance Doctor J was in before. "We've been looking at the wrong stats this whole time."

"Exactly. We have been treating her like a Transhuman that goes into a coma when their genetics malfunction, but all this time, she's been in a period of evolution."

"So, she was induced?"

"Yes. To trigger her mutation."

"Fascinating." Her voice left her in a low key gasp. "It's like a metamorphosis. It's almost like her own brain is shortening the distance between neurons." She clicked on the keyboard, almost pushing Doctor J out of the way. "But how?"

"Well, I can't explain it, but Miguel here is the missing link. Our patient found a way to connect with his brainwaves and send a message."

Doctor Sharp looked at Miguel, smiling in awe. Miguel had never seen her smile.

"And what's the message?"

"We must wake her. Otherwise, the mutation will continue. I've started the process to wake her, but I need your help and your guidance in assessing the damage."

"Oh, doctor." She made a pause. "I'm afraid the damage..." Jessica Sharp cleared her throat and glanced at Miguel for an instant as if measuring her words. "Nurse, please accompany Mister De Santos out of the room."

Miguel felt like she had just stabbed him in the gut. Why wouldn't she say it in front of him? Were they too late to help?

"Wait," Miguel spoke up as the nurse came his way. "Please, just tell me if she'll be okay."

Silence settled in the room, and Miguel could see how both doctors searched for words to deliver the news. Before any of them could say anything, a sharp pain on the side of his head blinded him. The surrounding lights flashed brighter, and all he could see were white auras. His legs weakened under him, and he fell to the ground. The sounds got mixed up in an echoing cacophony. The only relevant sound was the beep of Daiyu's pulse.

The beep quickened before it flatlined.

CRIMSON_

The cold broke the air as they descended to the Clover Holding Facility. At three AM, the only sound in the facility was their boots marching to a common goal. The Delta team had spent the whole night drafting the contract for 0397, and they were now headed to get him to sign it. Alyssa's heart hammered in her chest as she followed Commander Fox through the holding facility's hall.

They walked past the double wall mirror where it all started. Just three weeks ago she had been standing in front of that mirror waiting to get clearance to enter the lime room and prep it for Fox's interview. Had any of them expected this case to lead them here?

Alyssa was certain that nothing she did back then would have led to this if it wasn't because of her Unit Recommendation and the conversation she'd had with Esteban in the cafeteria. They started with a case that was bigger than what they had handled before, and nothing promised them it would be easy, but it was supposed to be straight forward. They were now on their way to ask their suspect to sign a contract under Fox in an effort to protect him from the board.

This was on the lines of betrayal.

They reached the end of the prep area, where suspects were held for interrogation and where they waited until a cell had been assigned to them. They now stood in front of the gate that would lead them to where the prisoners were kept, the holding hall. Alyssa looked around, feeling guilty. She wasn't supposed to be there. Only commanders and Omega bodies had clearance to go into the holding hall. Her wandering eyes stopped when they spotted a security camera hanging in the corner of the hall. She ignored the consequences there would be, but there was now physical proof that she'd been there, going behind the board's back.

Fox pulled his own identification card and scanned it at the gate. They waited for the machine to read his data.

"It will be best if the three of you speak to him without me," Fox spoke, his low voice still managed to echo in the hall. "After the interview, he might be less cooperative if he sees me."

Alyssa nodded. To help 0397, he'll have to trust them and their plan. She hoped sending her in wouldn't be a problem. After all, she brought him in.

"We cannot leave here without that signature," Fox continued. "We've already sacrificed too much to get it, and there's no turning back. When you talk to the suspect, tread carefully. The wrong word could cost us everything."

The electric gate beeped and rattled open.

Alyssa straightened up and gave the security camera a last defying look before she followed the rest of her team across the gate. As she walked through the halls of the holding area, she felt like she was burning the bridge that would lead her back home. She kissed her old life goodbye, perfectly content in knowing she'd never be able to rebuild that bridge. There were more important things to fight for right now.

The cell was not bigger than a broom closet. The air smelled heavy of bleach and felt more like a hospital room than a holding cell. It had white walls, a ceramic floor, and came with a bed, small washing facilities, and a tiny table and chair. None of the cells came with windows.

The spaces were meant to be used for a few days; suspects were usually held in the main Clover Building for a few days and transferred out to the bigger holding estates. Due to the case's complex nature, 0397 had been held there for what Alyssa imagined must have been an unprecedented amount of time. 0397 had been in that tiny room for three weeks, and by the looks of it, he'd been forced to acclimate to the room to meet his needs himself.

They found the flimsy bed frame on its head and relegated it against a wall. Alyssa pictured 0397 using it to exercise, and leaving up there to make more space. He hadn't bothered to take the thin mattress off the bed frame, as it rested trapped between the bed frame and the wall. Alyssa wondered if 0397 simply slept on the floor.

0397 stood from his tiny table when he saw them walk in. What was he doing up at three in the morning? Alyssa felt they had just interrupted something.

He looked better than the last time she'd seen him, but not well. His navy blue jumper looked crisp and ironed, his face was clean-shaven. Alyssa didn't miss the black inhibitor collar around his neck. It was an ugly metallic thing with a red square blinked announcing it was on. The collars both hindered most GENE abilities and zapped the wearer with an electrical charge if they decided to try and use any of the abilities the collars weren't able to suppress. Alyssa imagined that 0397 might be made weaker, or that at least he got electrocuted whenever he'd try to use his arm. He had black marks around his neck and over his arms. Were those burns from the inhibitor collar and the cuffs he wore before?

Under the white lights of the cell, his features looked angular and sharp, like a face chiseled from cold stone. The black eye that settled on his face and the cut over his lip were nowhere to be seen. The cuts and bruises on the rest of his body seem to have disappeared as well. It was clear then that he healed faster than a normal person would, yet another similarity with Transhumans.

0397's eyes examined them all. When they settled over her, Alyssa saw a glimmer of recognition on them, but there was still a hint of doubt. Beyond the cold gray of his eyes, Alyssa couldn't determine if he remembered her altogether. She couldn't tell what he thought of the whole situation. 0397 grabbed an old translator model from the table. Fox had probably left it with him so that he could communicate with the guards and the staff from the Psychological Department.

0397 mounted the earpiece on his ear as and with an expression that denoted both confusion and annoyance he said, "I've already told a commander everything I remember. You'll get nothing else out of me."

James exchanged a worried look with Alyssa. Not such a great start.

He cleared his throat and said, "We're not here to ask any questions. We've come to cut you a deal."

0397 cocked his head. He wasn't expecting to hear that. "All right, what are you offering?"

"A way to buy your freedom back."

"I'm listening."

James took a pause, breathing through the tension in the room. "The circumstances surrounding your case have gotten out of hand. We've discovered some people in the company would love to study your abilities and are looking to have you tried as a terminal case."

0397 raised an eyebrow at that. He could not know what that meant, but it didn't sound good.

"If we want to avoid them sending you to a research facility, we have to get you under our commander's protection. All you have to do is sign a contract to be under his command."

"You're asking me to come work for you?"

"Something like that. It is the only way we can help you."

0397 scoffed. He passed his silvery hand through his hair, shoving long strands of blond hair out of his face. "Help me?"

Uh oh. Alyssa thought. Fox had warned them to choose their words with care or they could have a situation in their hands. James had just hit a nerve.

"I've been here for weeks, telling people I don't know why I'm here. But no one listens, they just threw me in here and put this... thing on me." 0397 breathing agitated while pointing at the collar. "No one would tell me what's going on. For weeks. And now I'm supposed to believe you want to help me?"

"The way you've been treated hasn't been right."James put his hands up. "I understand that."

"I don't see how you can understand. I don't see you in here with me," 0397 added with a sarcastic edge at the end.

"You're right." James' tone was calculated as if he were trying to diffuse a bomb. "We're trying to change the way the company treats rogue GENEs—"

"Everyone keeps calling me that. Rogue. They say I lost control, but I don't remember a thing." 0397 shook his head. "All I remember from that night..." 0397 touched the side of his head, grimacing. "There were sirens and cops. I was bleeding. And then you came in." He looked at James, connecting the dots.

"So you remember our encounter? In the parking lot?"

"Barely. You brought me in?"

"We did."

0397 scoffed. "You brought me here." The confusion in his eyes turned into something else. "But now you want to help?"

"We always wanted to help."

"Oh, yeah? The way I see it, you could have just let me go."

"We did what we thought was best," James spoke, really enunciating his words, sounding stern. "You were out of control. You hurt people."

"But I don't remember anything."

"You keep saying that like it will change what happened, 0397."

0397 touched the side of his head again, in pain. "Don't call me that!"

Robin cleared her throat, as it appeared James wasn't going to be able to diffuse anything. "Maybe we should give the kid a chance to breathe, huh, James? We want him to sign the contract, remember?"

0397 turned to Robin as if suddenly remembering who she was. An aggression Alyssa hadn't seen in him since the attack in the Blue Flamingo burned behind his eyes.

"What are you even doing here?"

Robin turned to him with faux surprise and a hand over her chest. Her voice came out like a menacing purr. "You got a problem with me, Blondie?"

"Y-you tried to kill me."

Alyssa pinched the bridge of her nose, trying to stifle a sigh.

"Oh, that." Robin laughed. "Look, Blondie, you can think anything you want of me, of us, but we really are here to help. You think this is bad?" She signaled to the holding cell around them. "What can happen to you if you don't sign this contract is going to be a thousand times worse."

"Is that a threat?"

The light on 0397's inhibitor collar blinked as a warning, matching his heart rate.

Robin put a pleasant smile on her face. "Careful there, kid. You don't want to get zapped, do you? I'd calm down and listen to what we have to say if I were you. I'm half the reason we're cutting you this deal."

"Then I'm not interested." 0397 turned around and took his translator device off.

Silence settled among the Deltas. The chances of rescuing the conversation looked slim now. James and Robin pantomimed between them, reproaching each other for their callousness.

James looked at Alyssa apologetically and whispered, "You're up, Crimson Thunder."

Alyssa nodded and took a step forward from behind the rest of her Unit. The German that left her lips was stronger and more confident than the one she'd spoken with that night in the alley.

"How about we talk before you make a final decision?"

0397 turned back to see her, his gray eyes locked on her blue ones. His aggression cooled down. He remembered her now.

"Are you going to tell me that bringing me in was for the best too?"

Alyssa smiled at him sadly, "No."

0397 nodded. He left his translator device on the table. They understood each other, and he trusted her. "Let's talk then."

"Okay. I'm going to be honest with you, when we first brought you in, I thought we were helping you. When you said you lost control and that you couldn't remember what happened, I believed you, and I was sure the company would believe you as well. But I was mistaken."

0397 looked into her eyes, listening intently to her every word.

"The truth is, no one around here has ever seen what you can do. It turns out they are far more interested in learning how your abilities work than anything else. That means they are looking to send you to a research center. There's no coming back from there." For the first time since they walked in, Alyssa saw a strike of fear flash through 0397's face. "This contract really looks like the only way to protect you from those people in the company."

There was a spark in 0397's eyes that told Alyssa he had again just realized the complexity of his situation, but she could see an obvious and palpable doubt.

"The night we brought you in, you told me you were not done fighting. I can tell you that there won't be a better time to fight than now, and you won't be able to do so unless you sign this contract."

Silence settled in the room again. Alyssa saw how 0397 weighed her words and his options.

"You're right," he said, nodding his head. "I'm not ready to die. If this is my only option, I'll sign."

Alyssa smiled, relief washing over her. "I'll walk you through the paperwork, then."

TIGER_

Morning light filtered through the window walls of the meeting room and shone against the modest collection of medals pinned to James' shoulder. He wore his formal Clover military attire, a clean-shaven face, and all the confidence he could muster. That morning he and the rest of the Delta Unit had put on their formal gear and dressed their best for their last minute meeting with the board that Commander Fox had called—he'd said they had last minute information that would potentially impact voting on the 0397 case.

What the board didn't know is that there wouldn't be a case after Fox and his Delta Unit left that meeting room.

The Deltas stood tense at the far end of the room, waiting for the members of the board to finish going through the contract 0397 had signed.

A dry ruffle of pages coming from Madam Page, the chairwoman of the board, indicated she was done reading it. "What is the meaning of this, Commander?"

"What you are reading is 0397's contract to serve this company." Fox started his explanation but was promptly interrupted by the rest of the members of the board who were catching onto what they had done.

"You drafted the suspect under your service?" Alberto Bigagli's voice was surprised, but his expression was offended.

"I did."

After scoffing out a laugh, Mister O spoke from the far end of the table. "To what end? I don't understand why we're entertaining this."

Then you're in for a big surprise. James thought as he raised an eyebrow.

"He's frozen the case," Jim Rogers explained for the rest of the board, doing a marvelous job of looking like it was the first time he'd heard of this information. "By taking the kid under his command, he's protected him from any verdict we could have reached."

"Could have?"

"As his commanding officer, Millard Fox gets to decide if our verdict regarding the suspect is to be implemented or not," Mister Simmons, the Co-Head of the Military Department with a seat in the UK branch, continued for Rogers. The rest of the board was looking at them for answers as they were the liaisons with the Military Department. "Our ruling is as good as obsolete in anything regarding 0397."

Silence fell on the room, and all the board members looked at Fox for answers. James felt the tension in the room rise. It was suffocating.

Fox cleared his throat. "We have reason to believe the suspect in this case has been compromised. My Unit has presented evidence to prove that 0397 is a worthy candidate for our rehab programs. Nevertheless, there's a high chance that 0397 would have ended up in Hart Island in a matter of months regardless of your ruling."

All the board members started talking among each other in disbelief.

"Silence," the chairwoman demanded, not raising her voice. "How is this possible?"

"We believe someone in this room has the ability to manipulate the current terminal cases system at the Garden City Facility. This was the only way we could think of protecting the suspect and the company's best interest."

"This is outrageous!" Mister Bigagli exploded. "Who are you accusing of such a thing?"

The rest of the board members exploded in protests and echoed the demand for the name. In the face of these powerful people yelling at him, Commander Fox stood calm and collected, waiting.

"Please, gentlemen," the chairwoman said to try to calm her fellow board members. "We cannot ask Millard here to name whom he suspects of foul play. We must conduct our own investigation in order to remain impartial."

"I can't believe we're entertaining this charade!" Mister O's voice carried more indignation than James thought it was natural to have at that moment. "If anything has been compromised it's this case. Millard Fox took it upon himself to go behind our backs and enlist an Enhanced entity under his ranks. And a unique entity at that. How can this be allowed? Rogers, Simmons: You should know the Military Handbook like the back of your hands," he said while looking at the heads of the Military Department. "There must be something we can do to stop this insanity."

Jim Rogers and Carter Simmons looked at each other as if trying to look for answers in a silent conversation among themselves.

In the end, Rogers spoke. "There is no precedent for something like this. Nowhere on the Military Handbook says that he cannot strike a deal with a suspect. Whether we like it or not, 0397 is now under the commander's protection."

Silence fell on the rest of the board members once more. Their faces had a level of incredulity that James had expected to see, but he didn't expect what came next.

The chairwoman put the copy of the contract on the table and stood up. The rest of the board members looked at her, waiting for answers. "If there's nothing more to do, then we're done here," she explained as she took her coat and gathered her things.

"Madam Chair?" Jim Rogers ventured in a small voice.

"You've said it yourselves. Our ruling has become obsolete, and I don't know about you, but I've got things to do." She grabbed her scarf from the table and looked up at Fox. "I don't like this situation one bit, Millard, so here's what's going to happen. You will vouch for this 0397 and take him through the right channels to get him settled with the company. You better find ways to prove he'll be useful. You can expect a scheduled evaluation of your new cadet soon. Got it?"

"Yes, Madam Chair."

"Excellent. Jim, Carter, I want you to kick off the investigation on this board and to revise that Military Handbook. We do not strike deals with suspects anymore, this isn't a law enforcement drama show."

Both men muttered an affirmative as the Chairwoman walked away. The Deltas saluted her on her way out with respect to the chain of command. She merely glanced at them on her way out of the meeting room.

And just like that, one by one, the board members started leaving the meeting room. The Delta Unit stayed in there saluting all of them as they left. None of them saluted them back or acknowledged them.

After Jim Rogers left, a soft, purr-like laugh reminded them

Mister O was still in the room. "I didn't think you had it in you, Fox. That was a rather decent political move."

So decent that it caught you off guard. James thought. Alyssa next to him shifted her weight from one foot to another.

"I suppose it was," Fox answered noncommittally.

"Too bad you only managed to buy the kid some time and that you had to sacrifice the careers of these bright people here to do it."

Fox merely stared him down with a stoicism that gave James shivers down his back.

"I hope you didn't think you can protect the kid forever," Mister O laughed again. "How long do you think the board will give you to show the kid's use? A year maybe? They will be busy with this internal investigation for a while, but once that's over, we surely will want to revisit this case. I'll make sure of it."

Mister O took his coat and made his way to the exit. The Deltas saluted him reluctantly, and he actually stopped to look at them, like they were pieces of rare art.

"If any of you ever wants to recover your careers, my office is on the twentieth floor."

And with that, he was gone.

Robin let out a low whistle. "Well, that was intense."

"What does he mean he'll make sure of it?" Alyssa asked, wrinkling her brow.

"We can expect 0397's case to be reviewed in a year," Robin explained. "He'll try to undo our work and try to send the kid to Hart Island again."

"Then we'll be ready for him," James said as he tightened his fists.

"In the meantime—" Fox turned to them as his medals jingled with his every move "—you should go home and get some rest. All of you. It's been a tiring time, and we could all use it."

"What about 0397, Commander?" James asked.

"I'll process him and get him released."

Robin clapped her hands together, "That's fine with me. Wrecking our careers and fighting for Enhanced rights on the same night is quite exhausting."

Fox smiled at that and turned to exit the meeting room, "Keep in mind that we don't know when our next assignment is coming. I want everyone sharp and ready to go when that time comes."

The Deltas stayed in the room for a second after the commander was gone. James took a look around. There was a strange sense of stillness in the room and in his chest. He felt like he'd been running in place, not really getting anywhere, and that suddenly he'd reached his destination.

"Let's go, big guy," Robin said from the door. "You've clearly been skipping on your beauty sleep."

James laughed and followed Robin outside the room. He turned at the door to find Alyssa lost in thought. "Aren't you coming?"

She looked back at him, and with a small smile, she shook her head. "I think I'll catch up with the commander and offer to help with 0397's processing."

James felt a warmth in his chest, and he wondered if it was pride. Alyssa had really gone from this element in his Unit who didn't want to be noticed to someone with a bigger mission than herself. Almost three weeks ago, she told him she needed to make her own chances on this side of the company, and it looked like she had just found how. He nodded and left the meeting room, following Robin to the elevators.

MIGUEL_

The pain stopped seconds after Daiyu flatlined. Miguel's vision returned. The medical staff rushed to their workstations, forgetting about him. Miguel's heart hammered in his chest, and a cold sweat ran down his back. Had he been too late to help Daiyu?

"Turning on the chamber's chest compressor. Nurse, give me the status," Doctor Sharp said as she typed on her keyboard with furious speed.

"Presence of asystole confirmed, doctor."

"Confirming IV access," Doctor Johannes said as he worked on his own monitor and keyboard.

"Give her 1 mg of epinephrine."

Miguel froze, and guilt fell over him like a bucket of ice-cold water. If he had followed Daiyu through the portal that first night, would she be okay right now? His heart hung on the sound of that flatline, hoping for a spike that would tell him Daiyu was back. He'd take anything that would tell him she'd be okay.

Daiyu rested in her icy prison, her skin glowing with white light. Just by looking at her, Miguel sensed her like he had in the shadow world. There was this energy coming from her that filled him up, something that called him to her. A spark of white energy shone inside the pod.

"This makes no sense," Doctor Johannes said from his station. "Her body has no pulse, but her brain activity keeps spiking."

He stood up and took a step toward the pod. Daiyu opened her eyes, glowing with a bright white light. The pain in the back of his head came back. The black pod hosting Daiyu rumbled from inside.

"What is this?" Someone asked in the room, and the medical staff stopped working in unison.

The pod's top flew out of its hinges and crashed against the opposite wall, breaking the green tile. The porcelain doll fell on the ground, cracking its forehead. Daiyu floated out of the pod. She stared at the medical staff as if trying to understand who they were.

Doctor Sharp ran to the comms system. She hit a button on the comms system, and an alarm blared out. She'd probably used the comms system to call security.

The energy from Daiyu churned inside Miguel when he looked at her. It was vast and pitch black. Daiyu lifted a hand with blue nails in the air, and the whole medical staff floated in the air. She pushed them against the wall. They struggled and screamed.

"Daiyu, no!" He heard himself yell over the alarms.

Daiyu turned to him and just stared at him. Did she recognize him?

"Let them go. They were just trying to help."

Daiyu cocked her head and floated towards him, the same dead expression on her face from when he had just met her.

Miguel turned to Daiyu and focused on the dark energy radiating from her now. The black ink floated around her in waves, rippling like shadows. He searched for the warmth he'd felt from the girl in the gardens. His heart dropped.

"Daiyu?"

With a look, she lifted him in the air, too. Her dark energy wrapped around Miguel's neck and slammed him against the wall. The air went out of him. He tried to talk, to beg her to remember him, but no sound came out. All the air drained from his lungs, but the energy inside him grew by the second. That energy was the only thing keeping him conscious. It was the same energy he'd discovered in the shadow world. It moved inside him, warm and alive. Miguel reached for Daiyu's invisible force, holding him hostage. Orange sparks flew around them upon contact. Miguel pushed his orange energy into Daiyu's, got himself free of her grasp, and he floated up into the middle of the room.

The energy in him was strong. He could use it to face anything Daiyu threw at him. But he didn't want to fight. He had come back to the real world to keep her safe. He'd made a promise to her and to Angel that he would save her.

Against all instinct, Miguel renounced the orange energy inside him. He stopped floating around the room as the orange energy left his body.

He watched Daiyu trying to fight back, intent on overpowering him.

"Daiyu, it's me. Don't you recognize me?"

She cocked her head again, her black energy diluting into a gray.

Miguel gave her a smile. "I made it back, and the doctors listened to me. Let them go."

Daiyu kept her eyes fixed on him. But then she did as he said. The medical staff fell to the ground, all coughing and gasping for air, but alive.

He took a step forward and held his hand to her. "You're safe now."

Daiyu took his hand and closed her eyes. All the dark energy left her. She collapsed, and Miguel scrambled to catch her. She was warm, alive. Her breathing was calm.

The cold of the stethoscope against his chest sent shivers down his arms.

"Breathe in for me," Doctor Johannes said as he listened to his heartbeat. "And now out."

Miguel let the air out. The pain from his bruised ribs wasn't gone, but at least it didn't hurt while breathing anymore.

"Very nice. It sounds like you are healthy, and you are healing faster than the rest of us," the doctor added with a smile before wobbling back to his desk, a limp still left over from the night Daiyu woke up.

Miguel thought about that for a second. After the confrontation with Daiyu, he was in such pain that he was afraid he broke a rib. It was only a week later, and the bruises were almost gone. The pain bothered him just enough to remind him of the incident.

Doctor Johannes looked up from his notes. "So Miguel, tell me more about that night. Was that the first time you experienced the energy you described before?"

"No," Miguel said. "The first time I felt it was the night I followed her through the portal, the one that took us to the shadow world."

"And was that notion the same as the one you got last week?"

"No, this time, it was stronger. It was like I could see the energy inside me and control it."

Doctor Johannes jotted some extra notes. "It's as we've suspected then. Your first mutation happened during the night. The time your consciousness spent in the shadow world could have induced the mutation, or maybe your body was already programmed to do so." He shrugged with a smile. "Either way, it looks like your abilities have woken up."

"They have? But what are they then?"

"We must run more tests to be sure. What your variation looks like and what it can do." A smile escaped him as he jotted down more notes. "This is such an exciting development, Miguel. You very well could be our first Kinetic GENE, isn't that exciting?"

Miguel gave him a diluted smile and tried to make his voice sound natural. "Yeah! Guess I have superpowers now."

The doctor chuckled before handing him his schedule for next week. "That's right!"

Miguel left Doctor Johannes' office and made his way to the Recovery Hall in a daze. He had expected that the doctor confirming his new powers would make him bounce up and down with joy. From the moment he signed his contract with Commander Fox, all Miguel could think about was getting his powers and finding out what they would be. So why wasn't he excited? Wasn't he happy that his powers had developed? He looked inside him, but the answer eluded him.

Miguel sighed, pushing away thoughts about his powers. He had more important things to focus on. Now that Daiyu was safe, Miguel had another promise to fulfill.

He slipped his ID badge through a reader, and the door to the Recovery Hall opened for him with a beep. He waved at the current shift nurse as he walked past her station. Daiyu sitting at her regular green chair reading with her tablet. She put it away as Miguel made his way over.

"Did you feel me coming?"

"I did." She smiled with her porcelain doll smile. "All the way from the elevator."

"That's more than yesterday." Miguel pulled up a short stool and sat near her. "Is the rest of your powers coming back?"

Daiyu looked down and shook her head. The power she had a week ago disappeared after she fainted in his arms. "Not yet."

"Oh."

"It's okay. The doctors said I just need to wait until my body recovers from the coma. When my body is healthy, my abilities should come back."

"Okay."

They shared a moment of silence, listening to the stillness of the room.

"Are you sure you are up to try this again?" Miguel asked.

"I'll be okay." Daiyu looked back at him and held his gaze. "Let's look for him."

Miguel gave her a slight smile. He looked over his shoulder to see if the nurse was paying them any mind. When he confirmed she wasn't, Miguel turned back to Daiyu and held her hand and closed his eyes.

Daiyu let a deep breath out as she pushed the energy out of her. Miguel received it and managed to make it grow inside him. He vibrated full of life. When it became too much for him to hold on to, he pushed it back to Daiyu, and their consciousness merged as one.

Images flashed inside his mind: the sunny day outside, the entrance to the Clover building, people rushed from one end of the lobby to the other. He saw images of an empty cell and a long walk across the empty holding facility. A guard with a four-leafed clover stood in front of him. Miguel looked down to see his hands: one human hand, and one made of a silvery alloy. A guard took the bind off and offered him a key to take the inhibitor collar off. The door out of the holding facility opened in front of him, and the guard made way for him to walk out.

The images rushing before his eyes stopped. Daiyu grunted next to him and withdrew from his hand as if she'd touched a hot plate. Miguel opened his eyes and found himself in the recovery hall again.

"I'm sorry, I couldn't hold on anymore," Daiyu said as she drove a hand to stop her bleeding nose.

"Daiyu! Are you okay?" Miguel looked around and passed her a tissue from a nearby table.

"I'm fine." She paused to catch her breath. "I think I pushed myself too far."

Miguel's head filled with questions as he reflected on the images they had just seen.

"What was happening? What did we see?"

"I think someone else stepped in to help. They've bought him more time." Daiyu let out a relieved sigh. "Now we just have to find him."

Miguel laughed, relief washing over him. A darkness lifted from his shoulders. He hadn't realized it had been weighing him down before.

For the first time, he understood why he wasn't as excited about having his powers as he had thought he would be. Getting superpowers wasn't the only thing left in his life. He had more to look forward to. There were people to take care of. Important people. And they were far more valuable.

CRIMSON_

After the hearing with the board, Alyssa never thought she'd accept a paper-pushing task again, let alone insist on doing so.

A week ago, she caught up to Fox on the way to his office and offered to help process 0397 for military life. Her commander nearly sent her away.

Alyssa found herself almost begging him to let her help. She'd worked on this case from the beginning, and it didn't feel right to just walk away from it after their meeting with the board. Fox gave her a curious look. He warned her the process would be long, but if she wanted to help so badly, she could. She could even be the one to deliver the news to 0397, both good and not-so-good. She had no issues with that.

On that particular afternoon, the Clover Holding Facility didn't feel so cold. She walked the empty halls of the facility with a vague taste of victory in her mouth and 0397's new life in her hands. As part of his contract with the company, 0397 would be given a new identity and all the legal documentation that came with it. He'd even get a translator chip of his own.

She just had to have him sign the paperwork she worked all

week to get ready. With that, she'd close her first case under the Special Response Units, and 0397 could start his new life.

Alyssa reached the facility's office she had reserved to finalize the processing of 0397. The office was a small space designed to have meetings about cases that needed immediate action. She knew that the space had never been used to sign an element in custody under Clover service. With any luck, it wouldn't be the last time a Special Response Unit was able to return a rogue GENE to freedom.

Of course, 0397 would still have a hard year ahead of him. Her only regret now was that they had not been able to get him scotch free.

Alyssa sorted out a few papers and looked at her watch. She still had about ten minutes to spare before security sent 0397 up to meet with her. Their department needed to do some processing of their own before releasing him to her. Upon inspecting the office again, she found a file box on the corner of the room. That must be the evidence box she asked security to release to her that morning.

In that box, she found very few items wrapped up in thick plastic bags. The cleanup crew had packed all evidence relevant to the Blue Flamingo Incident. She found what used to be plasma disks. They were now just small, round pieces of metal, useless as a weapon or anything else since they've lost their sharp edges. She also found the clothes 0397 had worn that night. A blood-stained tank top and ripped military fatigues were sealed away in separate bags. At the very bottom of the box, Alyssa found the only item she'd hoped the cleanup crew had stowed away. In a large size bag, packed tighter than any of the other items, an olive green jacket laid in front of her.

Alyssa took her into her hands and let out a sigh. She'd been wrong before. It wasn't a military field jacket. It was a Forest Ranger jacket, or so the embroidered logo told her. Over the right breast pocket, the emblem of a black wolf rested next to a German flag. Alyssa wondered where he'd gotten something like that. She examined the jacket further and found dried up orange stains left by the drink the convertible riders had thrown. The event that started it all. She hoped then the jacket wasn't beyond repair.

A knock at the door brought her back to the office. A guard opened the door, followed by 0397. Alyssa's heart gave a leap at seeing him entering the room. He looked like a completely different person now that he'd been given Clover-issued clothes. A fresh pair of jeans and a gray hoodie from the Academy fit him better than the navy blue jumpsuit. The inhibitor collar was also gone.

"Hi there," she said confidently in German.

0397's face lit up when he saw her, a smile in his voice. "Alyssa, hi."

"Please, take a seat."

He took a seat, and she did the same on the other side of the table.

"They're treating you well?"

"Well enough. They cleared me out earlier. Took the collar off."

They exchanged an awkward smile. Alyssa's eyes rested on the marks around his neck for a second.

She cleared her throat. "Good. Well, I came to get you set up. We just need to go over the new contract and get your signature."

"Okay."

Alyssa put the papers in front of him and explained it all. She went over the board's terms added to his contract and the details about his new life.

"The board accepted our terms, with the condition that you submit to the memory recovery therapy for a year."

"What happens after that year?"

"There'll be an evaluation." Alyssa's heart felt heavy as she delivered that part of the news. "If you pass, you stay under Fox's command. If you fail, the deal is off. Which means, well..."

"Hart Island."

She took a deep breath. "Yeah."

"All right." 0397 took the pen she'd left in front of him and signed. He looked up at her and gave her a smile. She must have looked worried, because he added, "It's okay. It's more time than I had before."

Alyssa smiled and moved on to the next set of papers. "That settles it, then. You just need to pick a new identity and sign a global ID. There's a list of names and last names to choose from if you'd like to take a look." She put a packaged translator chip on the table. "This will be your translator chip. It'll link with your language center and let you understand whatever people say."

0397 took the paperwork and read over it. He signed all of them and handed them back to her. Alyssa took his new Global ID and read the name on it.

"Angel Graves." A warm smile filled her face. "I like it."

"Me, too I know it's not mine, but it's a placeholder while I find out what the real one is."

"Well, it's nice to meet you, Angel." She extended her hand to him.

He took it, the cold metal of his hand wrapping around hers. "You, too."

"I have something for you," Alyssa said as she got up from the table and went to the corner of the room. "I asked the security detail to get me everything that had been recovered from the crime scene." She took the jacket and handed it to Angel. "I was afraid this had been lost with all the confusion."

"Ah, man." He let a low gasp out when he saw it. "I can't

recall why, but I know this is important. This is... mine." His voice carried a tone of self-reassurance. "You didn't have to do this."

"It was nothing. I just hope it's not ruined. I think a trip to the dry cleaners might do the trick."

Angel stood up, holding the jacket tight between his hands. Soft gray eyes looked into hers. "Thank you. For everything."

Alyssa felt the heat rise to her cheeks. She hadn't done any of this to be thanked. "No, it's fine. We did what we could. I wish we had gotten a better deal from the board. Honest."

"I'm the one that should apologize."

Alyssa looked at him, confused by the comment.

"I have a feeling you've helped me more than anyone would have around here. You and your whole Unit. This wasn't your job, and all of you must've gone through hell to get it done. I was too angry to see it before."

"Fair enough." Alyssa laughed, embarrassed by his words. "All right. Your orders say that you're supposed to present to Orientation. I'll walk you to the lobby. They'll tell you where to go next at the front desk."

"Okay."

They walked together out of the Clover Holding Facility and up the stairs to the Clover lobby. Alyssa enjoyed the silence between them.

The daily bustle of Clover life received them as they stepped into the main Clover building. They stood together at the edge of the lobby, the pallid light of a December afternoon showered them through the glass panels on the ceiling.

"What will you do after orientation?" Alyssa asked after pointing him towards the front desk.

Angel gave a dry chuckle. "I don't know where to start. I guess I'll focus on recovering my memories. Keep fighting."

"I like the sound of that."

"What about you?"

"Me?" She shrugged. "I'll wait for my next assignment, make some decisions about my career. I guess that's my way to keep fighting, too"

They looked at each other and shared another comfortable silence, the steps of Clover employees echoing between them.

Angel gave her a last smile. "Good luck, Alyssa Dietrich."

"You too, Angel Graves."

Alyssa watched him make his way to the front desk. A sense of calm washed over her. She made her own way out of the Clover building, thinking about that last question. What would she do now?

Alyssa thought back to the files still hidden in her desk back at the Records Room. She realized then she had not thought about those cases ever since she started working on the Blue Flamingo case. Her desire to go back home went away when she dove deep in this case. And she didn't mind one bit.

Alyssa smiled to herself, knowing it was time. It was time to bury the skeletons of her past and forge a new path. She'd bury the cases she never closed and focus on the new ones. She'd focus on all the rogue GENEs she could help. She wouldn't fight for her career, for her old life, or even for herself. Alyssa would fight because it was the right thing to do.

ACKNOWLEDGMENTS_

Like an epic hero, every novelist embarks on a journey when writing a book. Without the help of a guild of allies, they'd never be able to reach the end of their expedition. My journey wouldn't have been possible without the help of an extensive list of people, and this book would have stayed a hidden dream, forgotten in some drawer.

My husband, Manuel, was my biggest ally in this journey. He co-parented these characters, co-created our shared fictional universe, and has always been my fiercest supporter. This book wouldn't have made it through its first draft without Manuel's exquisite talent as a storyteller and the many nights we spent brainstorming this story. Thank you for pushing me to pursue this dream, keeping me fed, and for loving me so much that you took it upon yourself to read every draft.

In my path to publication, I was fortunate enough to meet many other writers, but none so magnificent as my writer besties. I want to thank Jennifer for the long plotting conversations in her car, her beautiful artwork of my characters, and for being my truest friend. I thank Mary for being my always-willing accountability buddy and companion to so many writing brunches and late coffee breaks. And I give thanks to Krystal, for sharing her plotting expertise, her passionate feedback, and for inspiring me with her own writing career.

I also want to thank the other hordes of allies I encountered along the way who helped shape this book into the best version of itself. Many appreciations go to the current members of my critique group, Fiction Crafters, who helped me to shape this book into what it is today. A big shout out to the editors at Salt and Sage, for guiding me to take this book to the next level. A very special thanks to Veronna and Adrian at Paradgim Shift, who did such an excellent job creating this cover.

And finally, I could not close these acknowledgments without talking about the people who supported me before I pursued a career as an author. I'm thankful to my family in Ciudad Juarez, who always celebrated my passions and my successes. I send a warm hug to my dear friend Atziri, who was my first reader. A big thank you goes to my parents, Carlos and Hortensia, for driving me to writing workshops and for feeding my curiosity for literature. I thank my brother, Rogelio, for his unwavering support and for being my greatest cheerleader. And to my cousin, Luis Rogelio, I send my biggest appreciation for believing in me and my dreams when I couldn't.

AGRADECIMIENTOS_

Como un héroe épico, cada novelista se embarca en un viaje al escribir un libro. Sin la ayuda de un gremio de aliados, nunca serían capaces de llegar al final de su expedición. Mi viaje no habría sido posible sin la ayuda de una extensa lista de personas, y este libro habría quedado como un sueño oculto, olvidado en algún cajón.

Mi esposo, Manuel, fue mi mayor aliado en este viaje. Fue el padre de estos personajes, co-creó nuestro universo compartido, y siempre me ha otorgado su ferviente apoyo. Este libro no habría salido de su primer borrador sin el exquisito talento de Manuel como narrador y creador, además de las muchas noches que pasamos pensando en esta historia. Gracias por empujarme a perseguir este sueño, por asegurarte de que comiera en el proceso, y por amarme tanto que te encargaste de leer cada borrador.

En mi camino a la publicación, tuve la suerte de conocer a muchos otros escritores, pero ninguno tan magnífico como mis mejores amigas escritoras. Quiero agradecer a Jennifer por las largas conversaciones en su carro, sus bellas obras de mis personajes y por ser mi mejor amiga. Agradezco a Mary por siempre estar dispuesta a acompañarme en tantos almuerzos de escritura y descansos para tomar café y hablar de este libro. Y le doy las gracias a Krystal, por compartir su experiencia en la trama, sus apasionados comentarios acerca de mi historia y por inspirarme con su propia carrera de escritora.

También quiero agradecer a las otras hordas de aliados que encontré en mi camino y que ayudaron a dar forma a este libro. A los actuales miembros de mi grupo de escritores, Fiction Crafters, que me ayudaron a dar forma a este libro en lo que es hoy. Un gran agradecimiento a los editores de Salt and Sage, por guiarme a llevar este libro al siguiente nivel. Les mando un agradecimiento muy especial a Veronna y Adrian de Paradgim Shift, que hicieron un excelente trabajo creando esta portada.

Y finalmente, no podría cerrar estos reconocimientos sin hablar de la gente que me apoyó antes de que persiguiera una carrera como autor. Estoy muy agradecida con mi familia en Ciudad Juárez, quienes siempre celebraron mis pasiones y mis logros. Le envío un cálido abrazo a mi querida amiga Atziri, que fue mi primera lectora. Un gran agradecimiento a mis padres, Carlos y Hortensia, por llevarme a los talleres de escritura y por alimentar mi curiosidad por la literatura. Agradezco a mi hermano, Rogelio, por su apoyo inquebrantable y por ser mi mayor animador. Y a mi primo, Luis Rogelio, le envío mi mayor agradecimiento por creer en mí y en mis sueños cuando yo no podía.

ABOUT THE AUTHOR_

Born and raised between the border cities of El Paso and Ciudad Juárez, Monárrez grew up in a bilingual and diverse culture. With a passion for the written word, she set out to pursue a career in Fiction writing and graduated from Southern New Hampshire University with a BA in Creative Writing and English.

Monárrez considers herself a Mexican-American writer. Her roots and fiction crafting training in both countries gave her voice a unique flavor. Her writing aims to deliver stories placed in American settings that echo her Hispanic heritage through diverse themes, unique descriptions, and the use of magical realism.

Monárrez currently lives in Dallas, TX with her husband. When she isn't writing and stressing over her next manuscript, she can be found baking sourdough bread, geeking out about superheroes, or avidly listening to podcasts.

Join her newsletter here: https://www. michellemonarrez.com/

facebook.com/CloverTrooper

instagram.com/clovertrooper

Lightning Source UK Ltd.
Milton Keynes UK
UKHW010739170920
370068UK00002B/560